Cactus Wine *and* The Relic Hunters

Lowell Lee

authorHOUSE

AuthorHouse™
1663 Liberty Drive
Bloomington, IN 47403
www.authorhouse.com
Phone: 833-262-8899

Published by AuthorHouse 04/22/2021

ISBN: 978-1-6655-2265-6 (sc)
ISBN: 978-1-6655-2264-9 (hc)
ISBN: 978-1-6655-2266-3 (e)

Library of Congress Control Number: 2021907588

Print information available on the last page.

Chapter 1

Going Home

About a month before my retirement from the US Navy, I was contacted by a friend whom I had known from my second tour in Vietnam. Dan, a liquor salesman, had debriefed me every time I made my weekly trip with the Civic Action Team to take medical aid to the people in the villages outside the city of Da Nang. My job had been to count people with battle injuries who lived in the villages and report back on my medical treatments. Dan was always in my office at the White Elephant, headquarters for the naval support activity in I Corp, waiting for my report.

Dan called me in Newport and said, "If you stop by Washington, give me a visit. I could give you and your wife, June, retirement jobs." We both had active security clearances to secret. On our next visit, Dan arrived with a friend whom he had told me I would remember. That friend was Dave, the survey party leader I had known when I had taken time off from the navy to care for my mother. We had surveyed almost all southern Arizona. So, June and I met with Dan and Dave to talk about what the job would be, and they told us that we were to keep quiet about this project in the Arizona desert.

After our retirement party, June and I packed our household items and shipped them to Ajo. Then we went to Washington, DC, for our final review and to learn the details of our project, which took place at the US Naval Station in Newport. June and I had retired from the navy and were going to Washington at the request of an old acquaintance whom I knew only as Dan, a salesman I had come to know in Vietnam. Dan was working

1

for the CIA, and he said he had a job for which I should take the time to interview. It would allow me a good retirement at my home in Arizona.

June and I arrived in DC the evening after our party and our sendoff to retired life. We both went to the final interview, which was brief, with the Department of Interior, Indian Affairs, Wildlife, and Antiquities. Attending along with us was Dan, who headed the survey team I had served on with the United States Geological Survey, or USGS. He also was a former navy hospital corpsman. At the end of the interview, June and I were hired for the job in Arizona. We were warned not to tell anyone what we would be doing, as that would come out someday in the future. On our way out of the building, we received our photo IDs and employment documents, and additional information would be sent to our Ajo address.

We went to New Orleans for a quick visit with my sister's family. We stopped overnight in Gretna, Louisiana, and enjoyed a one-day family reunion. It was short because my sister had to go on a trip to upgrade her teaching credentials. So, then we were on our way through Texas, stopping at Van Horn, and then on to Tucson, where we spent the night before crossing the reservation.

As we crossed the reservation, the ring around the sun thickened all day long until it filled the turquoise blue of the Arizona sky. Storms in the dry country are infrequent but heavy—and this surely meant a storm. I remember this as the monsoon season—hot and dusty, but with occasional wind and rain. We started out at sunup, riding across the reservation over bad roads, down and out of the sandy gullies along the base of the mountain.

Even the coming of autumn dusk could not subdue the color of this land. Shadows here were not gray or black, but violet and purple. The crumbling adobe walls were laced with strings of crimson peppers, a vivid memory from my years past.

June and I were just passing Covered Wells when we came upon a Papago man hitching a ride. He had a stolid Indian face, at first glance, as he came out of the desert. Then he said, "Ride," and the dark little man lit up with a wonderfully genial smile. He had a Spanish bearing, a certain native grace, and an air of chivalrous gallantry, which distinguished him from more cold-blooded Americans.

June asked, "Where to?"

He answered, "Pisin Mo'o. Take Road 21 south." As we approached the intersection, he alerted me to go slow and turn to the left. It is just a few miles.

The old Papago introduced himself: "My name is Pete Garcia."

"I'm Russ Philips," I said, "and this is my wife, June. My mother, Jane Philips, was a nurse at the company hospital in Ajo from 1939 to 1956. She worked in the delivery room helping with Indian and Mexican babies, the births that the doctors wouldn't do."

Pete said, "My wife knew your mother and loved her. I know your father and helped on his drill in the Ajo Mine."

I drove down SR 86, watching for the Road 21 turnoff south toward Pisin Mo'o. SR 86 meets SR 85 at Why, from where you can go south to Sonora of Old Mexico or north through Ajo and then on to Phoenix.

Pete told his story of the cactus wine and asked, "Do you know of this story?"

I said, "Yes, it has something to do with cactus wine."

The old Indian said, "I have a tale you would want to know about in this area. We can finish it by the time we reach my home. I will tell you the whole story on the way to Pisin Mo'o."

This is the story that Pete Garcia told me.

* * * * *

"Deep in the southwest desert is a small group of villages named for the Kuk, the Ko-Lohdi people, who live there. They are so far off the traveling trails that one would be hard-pressed to find them on any map. The main villages, which are approximately ten miles apart, are Pisin Mo'o, Kohm Wo'o, Go Vo, and Kuhpik.

"The US Army had planned to build a railroad station around Go Vo around 1856, but they abandoned that plan a few years later and decided to locate the station farther north on the Gila River. The abandoned camp facilities, which included a barn, blacksmith's shop, two large wooden water tanks, about twenty whiskey barrels, and an old wooden warehouse, were given to the local population.

"One of the wooden wine barrels found in the old army warehouse had a label burned on it with these words in Latin: *In vino veritas, in aqua sanitas*. It was decided to age the tribe's sacramental wine in that one barrel.

The other barrels were used to age the cactus wine that was to be sold to the miners and travelers.

"The old warehouse had been brought to the village by wagon, board by board, using four heavy haulers with twenty mules each. "Pete stated that he was glad that he was not around for that trip." This lumber was from the forest of the United States.

"Shortly after receiving these gifts from the army, the locals renamed the facilities Gihgi Kihhin in honor of a village leader of that same name. Chief Gihgi Kihhin was a short, obese man who ruled with an iron hand and did not like to be crossed. Some villagers said the facilities were named not in honor of him, but because of their similarity to his body shape.

"The native women earned a small but steady income by basket weaving and pottery making. Some of the women workers of the village were busy weaving baskets for Chief Gihgi. Other women were laying out pots from long strands of clay, which they pressed together with their expert fingers and hands, knowing that the chief would be pleased with their work.

"The native women also ran a winery housed in a forty-by-sixty-foot adobe building in Pisin Mo'o. They made two types of wine, one for everyday drinking, and the other containing a mushroom for religious communion, divination, and their sacred, healing, and hallucinogenic powers. The almost inexhaustible supply of sweet cactus fruit provided the raw material for the everyday drinking wine, and a special cactus was used for the other, opening a pathway to the deities.

"During the Moon Ko'ok Mashad, the flowers disappeared, and the saguaro cactus began to make fruit. The year began when the village started harvesting the fruit from many types of cactus. The pickers, mostly women and children, gathered the fruit and placed it in baskets to take to the winery. A few select men would put the fruit in the pots and jars made by the women, which made it easy to transport the wine around the villages for the use of the people. This also helped with the trade between the miners, Mexicans, and other Indians.

"It's important to note that the women were the labor force for the villages. The men had traditionally been warriors, although they did not like to fight and preferred to move rather than get hurt or killed. When they had no choice, however, they would send out a small war party of about six special warriors trained in night fighting, who would usually kill the enemy in their sleep before the sun came out of the darkness. Those were elite strike teams—in and out at the break of dawn.

"The sand people of the desert preferred to hunt and fish in the Gulf before doing any hard work. The villagers all worked to prepare the containers for the cactus wine, making red clay pots and weaving many baskets to hold the sweet, aromatic nectar produced by the winery. Because of its 40 percent alcohol content, this wine could cause a person's eyes to cross. It was packaged in plain clay bottles for local consumption and wrapped in baskets for export to the outer villages. All in all, most people agreed that the wine was the most wonderful nectar made anywhere. American miners, who took a liking to it, called it Pisin Mo'o's Fancy Nectar. The name stuck and was printed on the labels of the handmade clay bottles.

"In late 1909, war clouds loomed from the south. Mexican bandits were raiding north of the border in Arizona and New Mexico Territory, to get money and guns for their revolution.

"The great Chief Gihgi Kihhin was a chief of the Hia C-ed O'odham, or Sand Dune People, also known as Areneños, Sand Papagos, or Sand Pimas. Hia C-ed O'odham were traditionally hunters and gatherers who did not like to fight. They caught jackrabbits by chasing them down in the sand. They also hunted mountain sheep, mule deer, and antelope with bows and arrows and caught muskrats and lizards. They would often just lie around and have the women do all the work, though the men hunted and went to the Gulf to fish and get salt for the tribe.

"John White, a former general in the US Army, was a brilliant mining engineer who had a mine in the village of Kohm Wo'o with a small camp for the miners. A tall man with hair on his face like Lincoln, he always dressed in khaki, like all mining engineers and army officers of the day. The chief nicknamed General White *civi-cu:c mp aggreg*, which meant 'a person with long legs.' Chief Gihgi partnered with White to build a small steam-driven power plant from the materials left behind by the US Army. The plant would provide power for the village winery, but the chief also hoped to make some money selling power to villagers for their huts and to the miners for their tents and cabins.

"The chief knew that White would have to invest in the plan to get everything that old Gihgi wanted, so they agreed to help each other as friends and partners. They were both looking for an increase in profit. The chief's business was with his wine, baskets, and pottery. John White was looking to build a saloon, store, church, hotel with room for special services, and boardinghouse for some working ladies. Then a Catholic priest from Tucson arrived and requested that he be allowed to hold Mass in the church once a week. These three men happily agreed and started their adventure. Allentown was founded, named after White's grandfather Gorge Allen. Allentown was on the western side of the mountain, and Kuhpik was just six miles away on the east side.

"When several thousand people flocked to the town, the American settlers needed White's Hotel, and Allentown sprang up around it. The hotel, which served the best liquor in the territory, was one of the more luxurious hotels on the frontier. At first the small settlement consisted of the hotel, half a dozen houses, a few tents, and a post office. The general and the chief made a pact that the wine would be sold in the Allentown hotel and the twenty saloons in Kuhpik, but no jail was ever built. When thieves who had been stealing from stores and other places were caught, there was no law officer to jail and try the culprits, so the miners and other citizens held a meeting and sentenced them to receive fifteen lashes. The Pima woman with a cut on her nose was not put under the lash, but she was driven from the town. The man, however, was promptly and lustily lashed, after which the townspeople handed him five dollars in cash and told him that if he dared to again visit the settlement, he would receive a double dose of the same medicine.

"You may be sure that the rascal and his girlfriend did not return, and the community was no more troubled by thieves. We could leave all our property unguarded and yet not miss a single cent's worth of anything. Petty thievery may have been curtailed, but a hard look, argument, or the slimmest suspicion of a misdeal was apt to bring the hammer down on forty grains of black powder. Street fights and saloon brawls were as common as cuss words at a muleskinners' convention. Lawbreakers were tied to a tree overnight and shipped off the next morning to Tucson.

"When the priest discovered that his wine supply was gone, he went to the chief to get wine for his Mass. He asked for sacramental wine, and the chief, being a good Catholic, gave the priest a good supply of the tribes'

6

wine out of the labeled barrel. The priest read the label and knew he had the best wine for Mass.

"Wang Xiu-Ying, the Chinese laundryman—also known as Tommy Wang—was roughly five feet tall and weighed about a hundred pounds. A thin man, he wore a long braid of hair down the back of his half-bald head, and his hands were rough from hard work on the railroad. At some point he decided that railroad work was too hard, so he changed jobs and became the best Chinese laundryman in the territory—and he would be glad to tell you that, if you happened to ask. His hands slowly became all wrinkled from the soap and water and the ironing he was then doing. As a laundryman earning his money in a more respectable way, he became happy.

"Little Flower, the chief's lovely daughter, didn't like the Chinese laundryman because he was stealing her customers. He told the ladies to go harvest the fruit and let him do his work. Little Flower was about four feet six inches tall and about that same size around her middle. She was always carrying a laundry basket on her back and looking for miners' laundry to do. She always complained about the working white ladies and what they did not have to do. She also had an ongoing battle with Tommy Wang, the Chinese laundryman, about taking work away from her by washing miners' clothing. Little Flower was a real bitch, and she had a crush on John White and wanted him bad.

"A group of Apaches broke out of the Apache reservation. This Apache party was led by a warrior chief named Jlin-tay-I-tith, which means 'stops his horse,' but he was just called Loco. His father was called Chief Loco because he was crazy enough to trust the white men. Loco was always accompanied by seven to ten braves who had left the reservation to do exactly what they wanted to do—steal and barter for the best cactus wine in the world. Loco was just like Cipriano Ortega, except he was drunk all the time.

"Cipriano Ortega, a ruthless man, was the leader of a raiding party of bandits. He was about five feet ten inches tall and weighed 179 pounds, sported a long mustache, and wore a big sombrero tied down with a leather strand. He had a two-inch scar on his left cheek and was missing his left trigger finger, which he said was okay because he was right-handed. In fact, Cipriano looked just like the picture of himself that hung on the wall in the post office in Bisbee. He always wore woolen vest and tight trousers, and he had two pistols on his belt, two bandoliers across his chest, and a new American-made lever-action rifle. He was ready to raid for the revolution—and to rob for himself and his companions.

"Cipriano Ortega needed information about the villagers, the chief, and where the miners' gold and silver were hidden, and he decided that the saloon was the place to get this information. He approached the boss lady and pretended to be a Latin lover, making small talk, and asking questions that a bandit looking for gold, silver, and other expensive things would ask.

"If the border war got any worse, villagers would need to prepare to protect themselves. Once the war began, the miners were stranded for many months before they could leave and return to Ajo. In fact, except for occasional skirmishes between O'odham, Mexican bandits, and Apache war parties, the villages, except for one small incident, remained virtually unscathed throughout the war.

"Chief Gihgi became concerned about his beloved winery. If the Mexicans or Apaches attacked it, the entire economy of the area would be wiped out, so an emergency meeting of the village council was held. Since they were there, the miners were included in the council. After three days of ideas, insults, and suggestions, the general was hard pressed to understand what the tribe would do if trouble broke out. They claimed to fight only when necessary but run a lot better.

"Priscilla ran to the general after Cipriano's visit to the saloon, because she was sure that the bandit would be raiding the area soon. He had asked questions about the number of miners and if the chief had enough warriors to fight off a raiding party. Bill MacFee spoke up and said, 'Last week when I was in Ajo, Pancho Villa and his officers were there.' So, the general planned to defend the village and his business, but when he asked Chief Gihgi to get his warriors ready, he learned that only six warriors were willing to fight. Then the general came up with the brilliant idea of moving the winery to the old army warehouse at Go Vo. General White, Bill MacFee, and John Johnson represented the miners in all negotiations, which worked fine most of the time—although perhaps not so well for anyone other than themselves.

"Chief Gihgi went to the six bandits and their leader in the Mexican encampment before they had a chance to raid the winery. He was looking for a way out of a war, and he had brought with him a jar of wine, so they sat in a circle and began talking as the wine was passed around. After the Mexicans got drunk and passed out, the chief went back to the village and said he was sure the Mexicans would raid soon. 'We need to get ready to move everything to the old army warehouse in Go Vo where we and everything will be safe,' he said.

"Magdalene, the madam, always wore a red dress, a white feathered shawl, and a flower in her hat. She was the oldest and more mature, and she treated all the girls like they were her daughters. They got ready to move with the tribe and the miners.

"Work on this important project began immediately. They would move the winery from the adobe building to the army warehouse in Go Vo. The winery vats and all would be placed on the four heavy haulers and moved by forty villagers working as mules. The winery would remain in the new location, which would provide a solid foundation, and resume operations nicely hidden from prying eyes.

"The Mexicans, all hung over and unable to think straight, had no idea what had happened or what was going on in the village. All they could do was complain and have some Chief Gihgi revenge. Their butts were sore. The seven bandits and their leader in the Mexican encampment would be out of business for a while before any raid on the winery would ever happen. Cipriano could only curse the chief and his wine.

"After a few days of extensive work, the winery was ready to be moved to its new home at Go Vo, some three miles south of Pisin Mo'o. They decided to make the move at night in the moonlight, thus reducing the risk of detection by the Mexicans and Apache raiders.

"At about midnight on a Wednesday night, when the moon was exactly right, the move began. The front wagon, using only a small lantern, was gently pulled out of the old adobe building with the first forty villagers on the ropes. The remaining three wagons quickly followed, pulled by forty villagers each, and headed south across the desert. The trip was uneventful for about the first four hours, with the lantern keeping the wagons in sight, and the weather could not have been better. But then Mexican bandits became aware of the light on the first wagon and attacked, destroying the entire winery on the four wagons. The fire alerted the Apache, who decided to attack the Mexicans, as their source of wine was on fire. When the Apache raiders saw that the wine was destroyed, however, they departed.

"This is what happened. The Mexican leader was convinced that the miners were moving their gold and silver from the mine at Kohm Wo'o. He ordered the wagons to be captured and taken to Mexico, but the Apache interfered, and the wagons were burned along with all the wine and equipment. During the fight, the lantern was knocked over and set the first wagon on fire, which quickly spread to the other three wagons. The blaze could be seen for miles, which brought out all the villagers, and the Mexican bandits were captured. The winery blew up and was scattered around the desert.

"Apache party about what they were thinking about the move and the sound of the Mexicans fighting with the village and miners, and after the battle were complete on their way back to their homes. Meanwhile the villagers had returned to Pisin Mo'o, picked up a desolate chief and several of his prize warriors, and headed back to where the winery was burning. The chief was sick over the fate of his winery and vowed to kill the Mexicans if he ever got the chance. Later that morning, only calmer heads managed to keep him from carrying out his threat.

"The Mexicans surrendered without a fight. They figured that being prisoners of the natives was a far better option than being killed by the Apache. They were put to work and built a new winery out of the equipment that the US Army had left in the old warehouse. One of the water tanks was used to ferment the cactus wine, and the other was used to store the finished product in. The old warehouse next to the water towers was used for weaving baskets, making red clay bottles, and packaging the wine for shipping to the outlying villages.

"Chief Gihgi Kihhin was so overjoyed with the plan that he gave Little Flower, one of his middle-aged and overweight daughters, to the general as a reward, even though she had been moody about the general the first day. Gihgi said to the general, 'You have been such a great help resolving all our problems. I give you my daughter Little Flower to be your squaw. Take her and make many little Johns to run around my villages.'

"The general wasn't sure what to say, but he replied, 'Thank you, Gihgi. But the other day, I heard that the Arizona Rangers have a warrant for my arrest.' He then looked at the chief and Little Flower, fetched his horse, and got out of the country as fast as he could.

"Little Flower said, 'That is all right, Apapa [Father]. I will take the Chihino man [Chinese laundryman]. He makes a good husband. He works hard and does the laundry, so I can have many little laundry boys for the villages.' This was Tommy Wang's last fight with Little Flower.

"The villagers made several trips back to Pisin Mo'o for spare vats and other gear. Before long, the winery was back in operation. Output was not up to par, but it was working. It was an all-hands operation with everyone pressed into service, including the miners and most of the Mexican bandits. After a week of extensive labor, the new winery was ready to produce excellent wine. The miner's chief and bandits asked, 'How we are going to start over and make a better winery and distribution center? With the new location, customers will be coming from Ajo, Gila Bend, Sells, Covered Wells, and maybe Casa Grande.'

"After the reconstruction of the winery, the miners and bandits stayed on with Chief Gihgi Kihhin and his villagers. The miners stayed for the ladies and wine. Tommy Wang and Little Flower had a good business and prospered better than most. The Mexican bandits never left Go Vo; they lived well working with the villagers and always had the wine that they learned to love, the special sacred brand. Cipriano was the only bandit to leave the village, and he went back to Sonora to look for silver.

"In 1911, a group of missionaries arrived to help the villagers recover from the Mexican and Apache wars that had never really touched them. The first thing they did wrong was to tell the chief that the wine making had to stop. Sometime later a fire destroyed much of the town. The miners removed the boiler and engine and used them as a power plant for the mine in Kohm Wo'o. They wasted nothing, for the wood was cut up and used as fuel for the boiler. The generator was attached to the steam engine, and for the first time in history, all the villages had electricity.

"Today on the road to Pisin Mo'o is a sign erected by the miners: 'Sighted cactus, drank same.' The Mexicans were the most difficult to send home, for they did not want to go. Peacetime brought modern technology and progress to the villages. The natives could now market their Fancy Nectar to the American miners in Ajo. The increased profits could be used to buy imported booze, and the old winery would fall into disuse and eventually be engulfed by the dry desert.

"Old-timers like to recall the 'good old days' before the war and talk of the never-changing seasons, the beautiful villages with trips to the Gulf for fishing and salt, and the easy lifestyle of village life. I suppose the most vivid memories are those of the old winery and its liquid output. There was nothing in the world quite like sitting on a dry arroyo bank at sunset and taking a long easy pull of the sweet succulent nectar known as Pisin Mo'o's Fancy Nectar. The spirit of old Chief Gihgi lives on in the casinos on the reservation today. We must make a buck off the rich mil-gain [American white men]."

* * * * *

We talked all the way to Pisin Mo'o. When we got to his house, Pete's wife came out to see who had brought him home. She called me by my name, as she had helped my mother with laundry and cooking for our family of eight children. She had given me my first taste of cactus wine. After we visited for a while, I found out that she had named all her children after my brothers and sisters except for her youngest, who was named for my mother.

We were about ready to continue our trip to Ajo when Pete asked, "Would you and June like another bottle of this fine cactus wine? You might as well stay here for the night. The wind, dust, and rain have started. You will be safer here than stuck on the road in this storm." The sun set, and the sky was dark and scattered with lightning and thunder as the wind pushed the dust and water east. Pete said, "You stay here tonight. The big rain is starting tonight. The road to Ajo should be open by noon tomorrow—or maybe not, as the washes will be full of water rushing to the Gila River. You must be safe."

At dawn, June and I were ready to continue our trip to Ajo, but it was raining, and the wind was blowing. Pete said, "You can't go until the rain and wind stop."

I asked, "Well, Pete, can we have breakfast and some more of that fancy nectar?"

Then we heard his wife say, "Get back in this house and out of the rain."

As we drove away from Pete's house, I told my wife of the shoemaker and his lovely wife. "While in school, I worked part-time for the shoemaker—sweeping the floors, dumping the trash, and shining shoes and boots for Mr. David. I liked to hear his stories of the old town of Ajo and his father, Solomon David. He told me of his father's search for a lost gold mine in the Pinacate. I had many talks with my own father, who was well versed in lost gold mines. He was a prospector, and when I was in high school, he decided that I should learn how to prospect for myself. So, on Saturdays when I was not in school or working for Mr. David, I worked for my father in his search for gold. Every ounce of gold that we found went to pay doctors to take care of my younger brother.

"When I finished school, I went into the navy like my uncles and several cousins. After two years at sea in the navy, I returned to Ajo and went to work in the mine's ore-dressing department for my uncle Tom. Working in the dust of the crusher and the mill, I felt wasted. I had to get away from there. I went to New Orleans, where my sister was teaching school, and worked in the oil fields as a roustabout. I put in many hours rebuilding oil tank farms after that bad hurricane. That work was better than the dusty crushers, and it paid about the same. After a while, I returned to active duty in the navy.

"After my father died, I returned to Ajo, as my mother and younger sister needed my support. My kid sister went to college and became a teacher. I never went back to work for the mine. I became a bartender, working relief at three bars in town. With its eighteen bars, Ajo had a reputation for having eighteen millionaires. Miners and their wives are drinkers. I had a long relationship with the old drunk miners—and their wives while the miners were on shift. I heard many tales of gold and silver mines, lost treasure in the desert around Ajo, and other things that the wives told me about. But those stories are not for your ears, my love.

"When I was younger and still working for Mr. David, I stopped by the shoe shop on my way to work one day to see him, but he was in the hospital in Tucson. I talked to his wife, who said that I could have the map that his father had used for so many years. 'The dream is what put Mr. David in the hospital,' she said. 'Here, go waste your time and life in the search for that stupid lost dream.' She also gave me Solomon David's journal with all his drawings and notes from his search.

"So now I have my work cut out for me. I start my search for the lost shoemaker's gold mine, if it ever existed, and I hope to find it. Step one is to get a job that will allow me into the protected areas of the desert. I will be restricted to the sections of the bombing range that are not under fire from the air. To work for the national monument would restrict me to only the monument area, and Fish and Game would also restrict me to those areas."

So, I answered an ad and landed a job working for a topographical survey party to map the desert from Mexico to US 80 in the north, the reservation to the east, and Yuma to the west. My time in the navy and work experience in the oil field proved helpful. I had a government truck and all the tools necessary to start my search in the forbidden areas of the desert. My knowledge of the area made me a big help to the team. We started our project in October, planning to work through the spring and finish our work in the field office before the hot summer. According to my notes from Mr. David, we would be in the desert where his gold mine was located at the right time of the year.

Solomon David was a Jewish shoemaker who loved everyone and was helpful to all who came into his cobbler shop in Ajo. He specialized in shoes for the miners. When someone was hired at the mine, Mr. David helped those poor people acquire good, sturdy shoes for their many hours of hard work in the mine. He would take their old shoes and rebuild them, and if you ever wanted them back, he would sell them to you at a fair price.

When Papago Indians came into his shop, he would help them with chew shuhshk (boots) and shoes for the whole family. Most of these shoes were used but in good repair. Customers paid him with whatever they had—cactus wine, pitaya, saguaro fruit, pechita (mesquite bean pods), and other specialty foods that he liked. He even took baskets that the women wove and sold them in his shop. He was a good man, and the people loved him.

Old Lorenzo, a Sand Papago, visited Mr. David and gave him a map to help the shoemaker find the old Papago mine in the desert. The old Indian made a promise of gold and treasure to repay Mr. David for his kindness to his people.

Mr. David wrote, "So today, I start my search for this lost mine and the treasure told of by old Lorenzo. As I look across the international border, I see the thumb-like peaks that rise above the dull black malpais of the Pinacate Desert. They are the sacred shuktowak, the Black Peaks.

When I climbed with horse and pack donkeys up into the saddle between the knobby black peaks, below me shimmered the great Lianas arenosas (sandy), the fantastic sand-bound desolation that sweeps west to the waters of the Gulf of California."

Old Lorenzo told me that I must travel at the right time of the year. The Papago moon of Vihamik Marsat (October) touches mildly moon, the cold touches mildly and Jomali Suipotok Marsat (November), low cold moon. Or Jamali, Low or Uta Vaokat Marsat, inner bone moon, (December) the middle of the winter. This is also called Ku Suipitik (Big Cold), as we would avoid the heat of the desert, and travel and work would be easy. Old Lorenzo said that I should travel in those three moons (months) and that we must pack food for our donkeys and us. The map was marked with signs for water and food available along the desert trail.

He continued, "You can lead the donkeys through the pass until you reach the other side, and then you will see the water tanks provided by nature. Water your animals. Then proceed through the canyon until you see a black outcrop of rocks. Look to the east of this outcrop, and you will see white rocks. Proceed to the white rocks, where you will find the bell that the outlaw Cipriano left there after he sacked the Santo Domingo mission. The gold is nearby. You will find a burned wagon and maybe a bone or two, because many people have died for this gold, so be careful."

The following October, I was recalled to active duty in the US Navy. So, I put my search for the gold on hold again, knowing that it would stay lost until I could find it. I went to sea on a supply ship to the western Pacific, on my way to the war in Vietnam. The Orient was a nice place to visit, but I did not want to live there. Two years went by fast, with one spent at sea and the other spent ashore in Da Nang. When I returned to the States, I was assigned to the Naval Hospital in Philadelphia. I married my navy sweetheart, and after her discharge, we were transferred to Naval Station Newport, Rhode Island.

We retired from the navy in 1975 and returned to Ajo. When I was visiting with some old friends, we started talking about the lost gold mines and where they might be. We decided to go into the desert the next morning to look at some rock outcroppings and discuss their importance in finding gold or other mineral deposits, and we camped overnight.

I do not know what happened. When I opened my eyes, I wondered, *where am I, how did I get here, and why does my head hurt?* As I rubbed my head, I tried to remember how I had gotten into that predicament. My head felt like something had hit me from behind. I recognized the area as being southwest of Ajo in the Sonoran Desert, north of the Pinacate and east of Yuma. I had surveyed that area of the desert in 1965, making topographical maps for the USGS. I knew where I was, because the desert had not changed much, but what had happened to my friends?

I inventoried what I had with me—knife, hatchet, hat, and desert clothing, so obviously I had planned to be here. I needed to get to water before I became dehydrated, and then I could start my trek back to civilization. I tried to remember what our survey party had found in 1965, because that would help me find my way out of the desert. The hike would help me remember what had happened to me and why I had returned to that place.

I knew that I would be able to get water at Papago Well, just east of O'Neil Pass on the El Camino del Diablo. The road was south of me, as was Mexico's Highway 2. In fact, I could hear traffic on the road in Mexico and see headlights from where I was. My best guess was that the mountain range to the west was the Pentas, the range to the north was the Mohawks, and O'Neil Pass was south of the Pentas, with Papago Well about five miles east of the pass. Wellton would be to the northwest and Dateland northeast.

As close as I was to Papago Well, where I could get water, I knew that I should be able to get help from the Wildlife Refuge, the National Monument, or even the Border Patrol on the Devil's Highway. As I started my trek to Papago Well, I remembered that I had seen a large deposit of quartz, and I thought about Mr. David's map and journal. I took some time to examine the area, looking for the bell or wagon. As I climbed around the quartz deposit, I slipped and fell into a mine shaft, knocked unconscious. When I came around, I was shocked to find myself in the presence of some small people. I thought that I was having a hell of a hallucination, but all they wanted to do was help me return to the surface.

They told me that little people such as themselves were known by many names around the world, so they could speak all languages. Their gods had given them a good understanding of the world and protected them from their enemies in the outer world. But they said that I should never tell anyone about them, as no one would believe me. People would say that I was crazy loco, and then I would have no work or support for my search for the gold or my dreams. So, I heeded their words and proceeded slowly. I did not involve any of my friends, who had proved untrustworthy by leaving me alone in the desert. I knew that I would not profit from gold found on that trip into the desert and that I would follow a map on my own.

Here is their story of where the little people came from and why they helped strangers who came into their underworld. As I remember, it starts with the words, "In the English-speaking world, we are called Knockers. At the beginning of time, we were the Chichimecs. The Aztecs persecuted us because of our small size. They killed and ate our people in religious ceremonies."

This is the story told by the Knockers about when the Aztecs moved from their homeland and settled in Tenochtitlan. Huitzilopochtli agreed to lead them, and the band started out. "First, they came to our land, and they called us the sons of dogs and said that we Chichimecs were primitive barbarians who wore no clothing and ate lizards and insects. As was their custom, the Aztecs captured some of us, then sacrificed and ate us. Upon discovering that we Chichimecs tasted bad, however, the Aztecs determined never again to use us as sacrifices. We learned to piss and shit in the pot, which made our flesh taste bad. Our crap was too good for those bastard Aztecs.

"We Chichimecs called upon Camaxtli, our tribal God, who warned us of the Aztecs and the way they treat those whom they call enemies. Those of us who had survived were afraid for our lives, so we wanted to move back into the underworld where we had come from and remain there. God Zotz, the bat-god of caves, allowed our people to return to the underworld of the bat caves and mines to live out our lives in peace and harmony, if we were kind to all those who entered that world that was given to us by Zotz. We were no longer the fierce sons of dogs that the Aztecs had once known. The underworld has made us peaceful, and now we help only the lost or those in need who come into the underworld of the caves. Those who come from the upper or outer world began calling us Knockers, because of the sounds we make to warn intruders that they are not alone in the underworld."

When I arrived home after looking for gold in the desert with a bad headache, my wife, June, informed me that I had received two large shipping crates from my father's brother, who had been a prospector in Arizona. Along with the many boxes and bags in the crates was a letter from my uncle, Jack Philips, that explained the crates' contents and why I had received them. I was surprised, as I did not know that my uncle had died. When I opened the first crate, I found a trunk and a letter from Uncle Jack, telling me that he had found the bottle and glass on Squaw Creek in Bottle Canyon, which was named for its several bottlenecks. He had made this find at the age of twenty-five, while working on a survey party mapping the area for the government.

Uncle Jack wrote that the bottle and glass had been a lot of trouble until a dog found him and told him a story. The dog said he had been searching for the man who, because he had talked to a bottle and glass, had been hospitalized for hallucinating. Uncle Jack had then decided it best to trust only the dog and himself. He also wrote that one day he had noticed that the bottle, which sat in his kitchen window, was full. He had not filled the bottle, and his mother denied even touching it. When he picked up the bottle, it had said, "Drink," so he had poured some of the liquid into the glass and drunk it. That is when his visions from the bottle began.

From then on, when Uncle Jack drank from the bottle, he would get answers to his questions. His first question for the bottle was, "What are you?"

The bottle had answered, "I am called a Bishop's Pint. I was filled from the Holy Bottle from a stream in the place you call Florida. There are other Bishop's Pints in this world, and I have heard that the pope has control of the Holy Bottles from which he gets his knowledge and power."

Then Uncle Jack had asked, "How did the pope get his bottle, if this bottle gets its power from the stream in Florida?

"What happens to one bottle affects all the bottles," was the answer.

Uncle Jack's letter continued, "This bottle and glass caused me a lot of trouble until the dog found me and told me a story. I knew then that I was in more trouble than ever before. Not only did I hear voices from the bottle, but I had talked with the bottle, and for that, I was put in the state hospital. I knew that the talking dog would put me away for long time, so that was when I decided it best to trust only the dog and myself.

"I am a loner and prefer to keep my distance from other people, and I am uncomfortable being in relationships. The only relationship I value is with my dog, who is smarter than me and much older than he looks. He is like an older brother who keeps me out of trouble, which is more than most of my human friends or acquaintances do.

"We started the search for the Seven Cities of Cíbola, which was among the many legends that propelled the Spaniards into the far reaches of northern New Spain. The legend was an outgrowth of the Muslim conquest of Portugal in the early eighth century. In 714 A.D., seven Catholic bishops and their faithful followers had fled across the Atlantic to a land known as Antlia—a name that, incidentally, was the source of the name Antilles, which was initially applied to the West Indian islands of the Caribbean. Bottle Canyon is near the place called Háwikuh, the southernmost of the Zuñi pueblos in western New Mexico. Háwikuh was reported by Fray Marcos to be one of the golden cities, the smallest of which was larger than present-day Mexico City."

Uncle Jack wrote that based on the markings on the bottle, he believed the seven bishops had it with them when they traveled over the western seas in search of the Island of the Seven Cities. This is the message engraved on the bottle: "Use the contents wisely. You must re-cork the bottle if you use the water of life. Pour it only into the glass. May it keep you safe and in good spirits in your quest. Remember to use it wisely, moderation in all things."

The trunk also contained several old books and maps of various places around the world. This was written on the inside of the trunk lid: "I was searching for treasure in all the wrong places until I found the answer in the shot glass, bottle, and jade ring." The whiskey shot glass looked quite old. The label on the half-pint bottle, which was full and corked, said, "This is the Bishop's Pint, the water of life. Drink only in moderation and to be edified." The ring, which fit me, was gold with a jade stone setting. I wondered what all of this meant.

Then the second crate barked at me, so I opened it and let out a dog that looked like the animal I had seen thirty years earlier in the presence of my uncle. I then realized that this was the one thing he had had a hard time getting used to. They had been supposed to train dogs for pack and draft work, as well as for sentry duty.

The dog said to me, "This is the story of the Island of the Seven Cities, a large place that covers the world from the northern ice to the southern ice, from the sea in the East to the sea in the West. You know this land as North and South America, and it is large enough to hide the Seven Cities. In the place you call Florida, I hid the first bottle from the killers of the Seven Bishops. The other six bottles were scattered across the land by the leader of the killers. You, my friend, came upon one of the bottles in your travels in the West. You have a claim to find your bottle in a place called Squaw Creek in Bottle Canyon, in eastern Arizona a few miles from the city called Háwikuh in New Mexico."

I thought that I was hallucinating again.

Continuing his story, the dog said, "Esteban—Black Stephen, Stephen the Moor—was a native of Azamor, on the Atlantic shore of Morocco. He was the first African-born slave to traverse Texas in the search for the Seven Cities. He traveled from Spain to the west side of a very flat island and then into Texas by way of the Gulf of Mexico. Esteban was sold to Viceroy Antonio de Mendoza, who assigned the slave to Fray Marcos de Niza, a Franciscan. Niza had been ordered to Nueva Galicia, and he was to leave Culiacán in early March of 1539. On March 21, 1539, Niza and Esteban arrived at the Río Mayo, in what is now Sonora.

"Esteban was restless over the slow progress of the friar and his support party, so he was sent ahead as a scout. Separated by several days' travel from Niza, Esteban approached a place called Cíbola, thought today to be the pueblo of Hawikuh, and announced his intentions to make peace and heal the sick. He told the villagers that he had been sent by white men, who would soon arrive and instruct them in divine matters. The village elders, suspicious of his claims that he came from a land of white men because he was dark, and resentful of his demands for turquoise and women, killed Esteban when he attempted to enter the village.

"Hawikuh, the northernmost of the seven pueblos known as the Seven Cities of Cíbola, was just a few miles southwest of the site of present Zuni, New Mexico. Your Squaw Creek is just a few miles west of Zuni, and I do not know why the bottle was found there. Perhaps Esteban was using the bottle to heal the sick, and it was taken from his body. I do not know how he came upon the bottle, unless he found it in Florida when he began his journey to find the Seven Cities.

"My master, Fray Francisco de Núñez, used his bottle to heal the sick, both animals and people. I heard a story of a man who talked to a bottle, and people laughed at him and forced him to live alone. After many years, my quest has brought me to you, because you have the last of the Seven Bottles. I want you to help me return each bottle to its rightful owner. After all these years, I do believe that you are the rightful owner of your bottle. We must continue this quest and recover all the bottles. There are eight bottles in all, and we must bring them together to make the world a better place. When we accomplish this task, you will be rewarded with the secret of the Seven Cities, which I have learned during my travels in this world."

The last sentence in Uncle Jack's letter said, "We can do much good in the world as we travel together."

Things have been difficult for me during the past few years. After my father died, I thought my life would improve, as he had left to me all his worldly goods. I had my good name—the same as my uncle, Jack Philips—and stories about his worldwide quest for treasure. The only property that my wife and I own is five acres of hot Arizona desert near Ajo, the trunk from my uncle, and his dog, Silvanus, who wears a collar with many stones.

When I told Silvanus that I did not like his name, he said, "You can give me any name that you like." So, I decided to name him Stan, and he said, "I like that name. It is much easier to say than Silvanus."

Now that my wife and I are retired from the government, I have a quest to keep us busy. I could continue my late uncle's search since he left me with many unanswered questions. I also have two nephews, Jacques the older and Samuel the younger, who live with their mother. My brother—their father—was killed in the war in Vietnam.

The trunk contained many other things—maps, books, boxes, and bags that were tagged with their contents. The larger of the boxes held beautiful items such as rings, bracelets, earrings, and other jewelry that any lady would love to have. I also found many old Abraxas stones. On one glass was written the word *Bebida*, which means "drink" in Hebrew. Another box contained amulets, magic rings, and jade. Sometimes called the divine stone, jade was worn by the Indians in an amulet to preserve them from the bites of venomous animals and to cure many diseases. The trunk also held a bag of deep indigo-colored sapphires, the pale blue of which are the female sapphires.

We have a large box that contains what Uncle Jack called St. Martin's jewelry, counterfeit gems that he discovered on one of his trips of exploration. He had found that when he wanted to eat, he could pay for it by hocking a ring. History records that these counterfeit gems were first found on the site of the church of St. Martin's Le Grand, for which were named St. Martin's beads, lace, and jewelry. They were all fake.

I decided that I was taking in too much information, because it felt like my brain was about to explode. I would take this back up on another day. Meanwhile I could sort through what I already had in my mind. I knew that the last place my uncle had searched was in Pima County, and Ajo was in western Pima County. As I started picking things up and straightening up the house, I had a flash of memory of my father, who was always telling me stories. Here is the story that came to mind.

A long time ago, a rancher told my father a tale about the quicksand in the Gila River. While chasing a stray calf, the rancher had needed to pull the yearling out of the quicksand, and it had ended up taking most of the day to rescue the poor animal from that death trap. Father also told me of the time when a ranch hand and his horse had been pulled to the bottom of one of the largest quicksand pits on the Gila River—or wherever things finally stop sinking. His trail mate had been unable to rescue him from death or even bring back his body. From that day, people had started calling that place in the river Dead Man's Curve. No one knows how deep this sandpit is or how many bodies are in it.

I need to remember to keep my mind and eyes open when I am near the Gila River, to avoid joining the dead men in that pit. I have often wondered what my family saw in this desert. My mother told me that this place is hopeless and that my father helped support his brother in his quest for treasure that would help our family. Meanwhile, my father worked himself to death in that copper mine.

I do not remember everything that my father told me about my uncle, but I do recall that he was always talking about lost gold and other treasures in the Arizona desert. The maps in my uncle's trunk must be the results of his searches, and I knew that I should use them wisely. Mom had said that he had traveled to almost all the nations and islands of the Pacific. She had also told me that he spent some time in the Orient and brought back many beautiful objects. I assumed that the ring must be one of those objects.

This desert can be unbearably hot in the summer, and the rains start in July and can continue through August. Visitors need to take plenty of water and keep to the roads, traveling only in the area permitted, to avoid having a bomb dropped on them. When the sky is cloudy, the lighting flashes, the wind blows from the south, and the sun is setting, some people have seen giant scorpions and tarantulas, which are large spiders, moving to high ground to avoid flash floods. They say you can smell the scorpions when they move in mass. People should be careful about where they place their bedrolls at night when camping.

Some people think I have distorted thinking and unusual ideas inconsistent with prevailing beliefs, such as a strong belief in extrasensory perception (ESP). They think this because I have reported unusual perceptions or strange experiences that have happened around me and to me. That is why I trust only my wife, and she trusts me.

I am looking forward to life and experiences with this dog and the bottle. As I searched for more information on the Bishop's Pint, I found that it has some powers. When my dog found me, he said, "Please give me a drink." When I gave him a drink of water from the bottle, he spoke to me again, calling me by name. "My name was Silvanus," he explained, "until your uncle Jack changed it to Stan." I understand that it is important for a dog to know his own name. He told me that *Silvanus* was a Latin word meaning "of a Roman spirit of the woods."

This is the story that Stan told me about how he developed trust and friendship: "In 714, seven Catholic bishops, their faithful followers, and their dogs fled across the Atlantic to a land known as Antilia. These seven bishops, who had quit Spain during the dominion of the Moors, were looking for the Seven Cities of Cibola. My master was my bishop on this expedition to the Seven Islands of Gold. We landed in a small inlet sea on a very flat land and traveled through the passageway into the waterway between the islands. To the north and south, the area was covered with much green, and the islands appeared to be barrier islands to the mainland.

"We landed and were met by many strange people dressed in skins and feathers. Inviting the bishops to sit, they passed a long stick, which had a stinky smoking thing on one end, to each of the bishops and demonstrated that they should put the other end of the long stick to their mouths and breathe in the smoke. It was apparent that these strange people were better able to breathe smoke than were the bishops, and they found it amusing to see the bishops cough and choke on the smoke. During my long life, I have learned many things about these people, who smoke pipes and drink a foul-smelling drink that causes them to dance around a fire to the rhythm of drums and chanting of the people of their village.

"The landing party shared in this foul drink and danced with the villagers, which was their undoing. As they fell to the ground, the village people took their heads and danced in a fever. They also attacked the ship and killed all the Spanish people on board, sparing only the dogs. I now had a new master, who cruelly killed my companion dogs and ate them. When I saw this, I fled for my life. I remained in the area for a while, hoping that someone from the ship had survived, but I eventually found that they were all dead.

"The village leader stripped the bodies of all they had. The seven bishops who had set sail to discover the Island of the Seven Cities had found only death. Each of them had a bottle of holy water, and I took the bottle and glass that my bishop had in a sheepskin bag around his waist. Knowing that I could not trust any of the villagers, I ran away with it in my mouth and hid the bottle in a place that only I could find. Then I returned to the beach where my master had died. When I got there, the villagers were dying with many sores on their bodies. I wanted to retrieve all the holy bottles, but they were not in the village, so I started my quest for the seven bottles of the seven bishops. I had six more to find and return to the Spanish people.

"A few years later, on this side of the Atlantic, many dogs helped the Spaniards conquer the Indians of Mexico and Peru in their search for the Seven Cities of Gold. I believe you call them the Seven Cities of Cíbola or Seven Golden Cities. That was the same legend that brought my bishop and the others, who had hoped to find peace and a safe home away from all war and domination. Unfortunately, the only peace they found was the grave because there was only war and death in this new world. The natives Indians learned later to use dogs for their protection from the white man."

From the story the dog told me, I now understand why many people thought that my uncle was a crazy man who should have been in the hospital on Twenty-Fourth Street in Phoenix. He did spend a short time in that hospital, but I can only guess that the doctors and nurses must have heard him talk and then did not want to be patients in this hospital. I saw my uncle when he returned to Ajo after that vacation he had in Phoenix. Then he was off on another trip, prospecting in the desert and wherever he felt the need to go. I wished that I were as free as Uncle Jack had been.

I had opened the trunk and removed the items listed for an old Papago mine on the reservation about twenty miles east of Ajo. The map was marked as the Tarantula Gold Mine. June and I were having a difficult time getting assess to the site marked on the map in the Valley of the Tarantula, or what was now called Spider Valley, until we contacted our good friend Pete Garcia. He introduced us to the council and told them of my family history with the Papago Nation. Some of the members had known my mother and praised her for her work at the hospital in Ajo. She had helped many Indians when the doctors had been unable to help because they were too busy or had finished their shift.

Then the chiefs decided that only I could help their people. Jack Philips's trunk contained many things that were hard to find, including a map with the location of the Tarantula Gold Mine. This mine was near Ajo, and it had top priority. All must work for any reward. Sometimes everything is just about right, and then some crap happens and the chaos begins again. Then the challenge makes its appearance, and you know that you can overcome any challenge that comes your way.

Chapter 2

Tarantula Valley

Pete and I arrived in Tarantula Valley—or Spider Valley, *tokihtuD wo'otk,* of Papago legends—early on Monday morning. They started with the old map, checking the markings compared with the area where they hoped to start their search. Deciding to search by the grid, they marked the grid with piles of rocks until they could pick up some twine in Ajo.

Old Pete said, "Here, Russ, use this metal detector. It will help pick up minerals down about six inches. Angel and I found old guns and other junk and a coin or two just a few months ago. Would you believe it? Right there in my own yard. I also brought extra batteries." We started finding brass of the fifty-caliber type. That area had been used for pilot training by the Army Air Corps in World War Two, and then into the 1960s for ground support by the army and marines. I had known all about this when I surveyed the air force bombing range back in the sixties.

Soon June and Angel, with her son Manuel, brought us lunch and more water. After lunch we decided to pick up the brass and put it in piles, waiting to learn what the council wanted to do with it. We walked about a third of the valley as the sun was setting in the west. Then it was time for supper and a good rest, so that we could start again the next morning. Pete said that he would send Manuel to Ajo to get some twine and a larger water bottle, since his clay olla (jar) had so many cracks that we were losing more water than we drank. Also, no more cactus wine until the job was completed.

Russ and June Philips were on their way to discovering a gold mine on restricted government lands.

At daybreak, we entered the valley and noticed that the rock markers had been scattered. We knew that the dissenters had been busy in the night and the brass had been taken, so Pete and I started all over again. When Manuel arrived, he said, "Those bastards did their dirty work during the night while I was in Ajo. Pancho was in the store buying picks and shovels, and he told me that we would never uncover anything. Then I went to the lumber yard and bought these wooden stakes to tie the twine to, along with this five-gallon water container." Pete told his son that he had done well and sent him on another mission: "Take the pickup to our house and get a tarp—ten by ten, or ten by twenty—out of the storage shed so that we can have some protection from the sun during the hot days. Also bring some long poles and the ribs of the dead saguaro cactus in the back. By then, you and your mother and June will be ready to bring us lunch."

As Pete and I surveyed the damage at the working dig, we talked about how we could get some advantage from these wild Indians. I said, "We need to set them up so that they will go to the council to report their findings on this site."

Pete asked, "Just how in hell can we do that?"

I replied, "When Manuel returns with the tarp and poles, we can act like we were being the bad boys they say we are. We will start by shoveling some dirt and rocks onto the tarp at the end of the day. When we leave, we will take the tarp with its load of rocks and put them into the back of the truck. I believe that Pancho has one of his men watching us right now. He should stay, and after we leave, he will tell his master, Pancho, what we have done. I am sure that he will run to the council to inform them that we are the crooks that he said we are. But we will be there, waiting for the chance to deliver the rocks to the council. This should persuade the council to put a policeman in the area to watch for trouble."

Soon June and Angel arrived with our lunch, and not far behind was Manuel with the tarp and poles. We ate our lunch, and then our wives watched us as we took the tarp and cactus poles out of the truck.

When Manuel asked what he should be doing, Pete said, "Just do what we do. Pancho is watching what we are doing. We will stake out a four-square grid to work on today. When we are finished for the day, we will spread that tarp on the ground and place some rocks on it. Pancho will run to the council to tell them that we are thieves, but we are planning to get to the council before those wild Indians do. When we show the council the rocks in the tarp, we might get some night patrol in the valley. A good policeman on horseback might be able to catch them in their unlawful tricks, destroying the work that we are doing for the people."

The ladies, who looked a little confused, started asking questions that afternoon. When we told them our plan, they became afraid that Poncho's gang would take some action themselves before we were on our way home. We continued with the plan, however, making a big fuss over a few rocks and placing them and the tarp into the pickup truck. Then we picked up our tools, leaving the cactus poles behind, and the grid remained marked by all our shovel and pick marks on the ground. We all had a laugh as we left Spider Valley and returned to Pisin Mo'o, where we spent another night with Angel and Pete so that we could beat Pancho's gang to the council office in the Tribal District. Manuel wanted to go back to the valley with his brothers, though, just to watch over the workplace.

Pete and I arrived at the council office early, so we parked the pickup behind the building and walked across the street for coffee. Then we took our cups of coffee back to the council building and walked in, since it was open for daily business. When the chief asked, "What brings you here today?" Pete told him that we needed to speak with the council. The chief invited us into his office and asked, "What is the problem?"

Pete said, "We are having problems at the dig in the valley. Pancho and his gang are harassing us, and they took the brass shells that we were recovering while looking for the lost mine. You know that the Americans will pay you for all the brass they used in training their fliers during the last few wars."

While we were talking, Pancho broke into the office and yelled, "I see you have these crooks in your office. You need to get them off the tribal lands. They are robbing us by taking things out of the valley." When Pete asked what "things" he was talking about, Pancho said, "The things that I saw you load into your pickup truck when you left the valley last night. Look out the window. Your truck is parked in the back lot, and it has something in the back."

The chief said, "I need to go out and see what is in the back of that truck. Come with me now." As we all walked out to the parking lot, Pancho asked what was going on. The chief replied, "We are going now to see why we are all here. Pancho, how and why did you know what Pete and Russ were doing at that site in Spider Valley? Were you spying on them, and why did you destroy the site on the night before last?" Pancho was walking backward as he talked and tried to justify his actions.

Investigating the back of the truck, the chief uncovered the rocks that Pancho said he saw us taking from the valley. "Rocks under a tarp?" he exclaimed. "You've got to be kidding me. Pancho, I see that you have been harassing these two men who are working for the tribe. You are not to do that anymore." Turning then to Russ and Pete, he said, "I will see that a tribal policeman makes rounds in Spider Valley with instructions to arrest anyone found there. We will sort out these things the next morning before the council." Pancho did not like the chief councilor's words and was more excited than he would do more. In the future.

As we drove away, Pete asked, "Russ, where did you get these maps?"

"Maybe we should go to my house in Ajo," I replied. "I can show you everything, since we are brothers in this whole operation."

Pete said, "You make it sound like this is a military operation. Just what the fuck did you do in the navy for twenty years and in all those jobs that you traveled to for the last twenty years?"

I said, "Wait until we get to the house."

As we drove up to the house and parked in the driveway, Pete said, "Let's get into the house so I can hear your story."

I took him straight to the spare bedroom and then asked, "Pete, did you know Jack Philips, my uncle?"

"Yes, I remember him," said Pete. "He came to visit your mother and father twenty to thirty years ago. Jack was sent to the hospital on Twenty-Fourth Street in Phoenix because he claimed to have conversations with a bottle and glass. He had a dog just like the one looking at me through the door right now."

I said, "Don't worry. This is the same dog, and he is friendly." Turning to the dog, I asked, "You are friendly, right?"

The dog said, "Yes, I am friendly, and I do miss Jack."

Pete immediately sat down on a chair, stunned at hearing the dog speak, and said, "That is a good part of your story, Russ. I am ready for more."

I opened the trunk and showed Pete the maps, artifacts, books, bottle, glass, and rings. I said, "Look at this map. It is an area on the reservation right around your home, near Gunsight Ghost Town. This is where I got the map and the stone of the spider women. You do understand what is driving me, Pete, and if I am crazy like Uncle Jack, you are now in that same boat."

Pete said, "I am retired from the copper mine in Ajo, and I have always wondered what I would do with the rest of my life. I believe that you just showed me my future, and I like it very much. When can I tell Angel and my boys, as they are part of this new life?"

I replied, "June is telling them right now, so we should get to your home as soon as we can." Then I picked up the bottle and glass and asked, "Would you like a drink from these?"

Noticing that the bottle was full, Pete said, "Just a little one." So, I pulled the stopper and poured a small one for him. When he took the glass and lifted it to his mouth, the glass said, "Drink," so Pete did. Then he said, "It tastes like water, but it is more than water. I have begun to understand your quest, Russ, and I have a desire to complete this quest with you and June." We took the dog, bottle, and glass with us as we drove back to Pete's house and family.

When Pete asked the dog's name, the dog answered, "I was named Silvanus by my first master, one of the bishops, when we arrived from Spain many years ago, but later Jack renamed me Stan. I survived the killing of the bishops and ran away with my bishop's bottle and glass. I was found by Spanish conquistadors, and I hid the Bishop's Pint and his glass in the bag in which he carried them. We crossed this large island and found ourselves in Mexico. The Spaniards told of the large cities of gold that we found while crossing the island. My master used the bottle and glass for the natives who were sick, and we got safe passage through their lands. Yes, Russ calls me Stan, which I like better than my old name. You and your family should do the same. This will keep us all safe from the people who could use it against us."

When we arrived at Pete's home, we went inside and joined the family in the front room, where we took a seat. June said, "I told Angel and her sons about the bottle and glass and what it will do to help us in our quest." I then asked Angel if she would like to drink from the bottle and glass, and she said, "Pete has, so I must too." When she took the glass in hand, it said, "Drink," and she did drink. Then she called their sons and told them to drink water from the bottle with the glass, and because they were good sons, all three of them drank.

As June, Stan, and I drove back to Ajo, we all had a good feeling about everything that we had accomplished that day. The council was going to place a police patrol in Spider Valley, and Pete and his family were on board with us to continue our quest if we could. Sitting in the back seat, Stan spoke up and said, "Don't worry about getting old. Just take a good look at me. It will not take long for Pete and family to figure this out for themselves." When I suggested that we use some of the rings for everyone in our project, Stan agreed. "That is a good idea, and the power of the rings will keep us all just a little bit safer."

As I was thinking that Uncle Jack had done the right thing by passing the trunk to me, Stan said, "Keep it under control." I thought to myself, *I wonder if that dog can read my mind.* Then, although he did not speak another word, somehow, I heard, "Yes, I can."

Driving back to Ajo, I said, "We will be busy this coming week. I feel that something big will happen for the good of all of us because we are working toward the goal of the quest."

The morning seemed to come faster than usual, and it felt like we would have all the time we needed. We would soon find whatever Uncle Jack had wanted us to find. We drove in silence—June, me, and good old Stan, who broke the silence by saying, "I hope Angel has cooked something good for breakfast." When I asked Stan, who fed him when we were not around, he said, "Bob feeds me, because we are friends, and we look after each other."

"Okay, Stan, just who is Bob?" I asked.

"You know that cat that you see most of the time when you come home?" asked Stan. "She told me that her name is Bob-Cat, and her kittens live in that big box in the back of our house. You know, the box in which I came to you and June? I am sure that they are in their house out of the heat right now since we are away."

"Well, Stan," I asked, "how long has this relationship been going on?" June was laughing as I gave Stan the third degree.

Stan said, "You know the answer to that question. Why are you asking me something when you already know the answer, Russ? From the first day that I came to you, that poor cat was hungry, so I gave her one of the beef steaks out of that thing that you call an icebox. She left and then returned with two kittens. They were so cute that I could not turn them out into the heat. At night, she scared the shit out of the bastard who was trying to get in through that thing that you call the doggy door, and he left with only half of his nose. She is good.

"Then there was another thing. You know that neighbor lady who lives next door with the little girl? This big man was dragging the little girl to his car, and the lady was crying. So, we stopped that bastard and ran his ass up a tall cactus on the other side of the street. He was screaming as we escorted the little girl back to her mother, who was overjoyed at what we had done for her and the girl. When the policeman asked what had happened, I heard the lady tell him that the big man had gotten his scratches from climbing up a cactus trying to get away from a bobcat. The policeman said that it looked like the big man had pooped himself as well. He drove away laughing and saying that bastard that he would be cleaning up that shit before he was placed in jail."

"Stan, you always have a good story," June said, "but I heard that story in the market last week, and it was in the newspaper as well. I am sure that the courts will be keeping him away from little girls, and the judge did not like his story either. When the Phoenix news channel came down to Ajo to get a story about that rescue, nobody said anything, not even the little girl's mother."

I do not know what kind of conversation goes on between dogs and cats, but it seemed to be ESP—you know, like brain to brain. They seemed to be able to communicate with each other, and I think Stan did that with me at times. I was troubled by the relationship between Stan and Bob, so I talked to Stan about it. He told me that Bob wanted to go with us when we went exploring the desert, and that she claimed to be a good hunter.

I replied, "We need to make this request of the team when we are all together, Stan. The others need to understand that Bob would be bringing her kittens with her, and that you are behind her all the way. Since she can get a full-grown man to climb a cactus, she would be a good guard cat on our work sites."

When we got to Pete's home so that we could all go together to Spider Valley, Stan said, "Bob and her kittens are in the car with us, so we can include them in the team today without any delay."

When Pete came out to meet us and saw the bobcat in the back seat, he said, "So Bob is coming with us today?"

Stan asked, "Hey Pete, does Angel have any good breakfast treats for good dogs and cats?"

We left Pete's house in a convoy of pickup trucks and cars and drove up the road to the Valley of the Tarantula. As we entered our site, we saw that the stakes and grid had been removed again. We knew that this disagreement would lead us to a bad place, because we would not put up with Pancho trying to chase us out of this valley.

Suddenly Bob cried out with a loud voice and scrambled to get out of the car. Stan said, "She has seen someone out there in the rocks, up that hill to the right." The person started to run when he saw a cat and dog coming after him at a fast run. Bob took him down, with Stan was right behind the fast cat, and they held him down until Pete and I caught up and took over. Stan warned me that a man on horseback was headed our way, and I said, "It is a tribal police officer coming to check out the site and make an arrest."

Then Pete and I said together, "Stan and Bob, you make a good team. You saw trouble and reacted like team members should always do." Looking down at the Indian, I saw that he was Diego Martinez, one of Pancho's men.

When the policemen arrived, he said, "Hi, Pete, I see that you got him. Diego, where is the horse that you were riding when I saw you earlier? Without a horse, it will be a long walk to the jailhouse."

Stan said to me, "I told you that Bob is a good cat to have around. You are going to give her a drink out of the glass from the good bottle, right?"

I turned to Pete and asked, "Pete, should we give Bob a drink?"

Pete said, "Why not give everyone a shot? We are only eight now, and nine would be better. Cats have nine lives, don't they?"

As we sat in a circle, I asked, "Bob, do you want to join us on this quest to find the treasures that my uncle Jack started?" Bob walked up to me and licked the glass, so I said, "Here, Bob, I will pour some of the water from this bottle into this small glass that you just licked, and then you will have some of this water of life." Bob then put her tongue into the glass and drank it all in one lick, then walked back and sat with Stan.

When I said, "Let's get to work," Bob ran over to her kittens, sniffed, and licked them, and then began her patrol around our project. Pete said, "I guess she knows her job. She must be the first watch cat on a digging project."

So, we all started our search. June and Angel, along with her youngest son, worked on the tent where we would take breaks for water and shade. Others of us began the hard work of digging into what we thought was a mine, extending into the mountain, which had been closed with the rocks easily found all around the valley. Such rocks were noticeable because of their different colors. "Look here, Pete," I said, "the rocks on the ground are black on top, but when we turn them over, they have white bottoms. But some of the rocks here on this pile have their white bottoms showing, so someone used them to hide something." Pete called Mike and John, his two older sons, to get their gloves and help move those rocks out of the hole in the mountain.

We started with a long iron bar, probing, and moving the top rocks so that we could get to the larger stones. That was the hardest work I have ever done. Pete knew what it was like to work hard in the heat of the Ajo mine. As I watched his sons, I could tell that he was a good father who had taught his boys a strong work ethic.

Suddenly Mike called out, "There are mine supports in this hole. Looks like ironwood and mesquite, so this must be what we are looking for."

Hearing the commotion, we were making, the women came over and asked, "What are you all shouting about?"

John answered, "We found what looks like an old mine. It looks like it may take some time to move all these rocks. We'll need to support the tunnel, so that we can get inside to see if this is the Spider Mine."

"Look at the big spiders coming out from among those rocks in the hole," Angel exclaimed.

Pete said, "Oh hell, this must be their nest. What are we to do about the spiders while we move the rocks?"

"Let us go over to the tent," I suggested, "and discuss what to do about the spiders."

Then Stan spoke up and said, "Here's my suggestion: Don't do anything. Let the bottle do its job, and everything will be okay. They know why we are here. They will stay out of our way and not let anybody interfere with our work."

"How do you know that?" asked John.

Stan replied, "I speak spider as well as cat, so let the bottle do its thing."

"I feel sorry for Pancho and the rest of his gang," said Mike. "Now it's not only us, but also the dog, cat, and all those spiders."

So, we went back to work on the mine entrance, moving the rocks about thirty feet away from the entrance, as we did not know how many rocks blocked the mine.

Mike said to Pete, "Dad, this could take weeks. You know that I need to get back to the university in January."

"You will be able to get back to class soon," I said. "Look through this hole in the rock plug."

Using his flashlight, Mike saw what I had seen. "It looks like a room behind these rocks," he exclaimed.

We decided it was time to take a break. As we came out of the mine, the women asked, "What now? Is there another problem?"

I answered, "Yes, we need to start shoring up the mine entrance so we can work safely."

"We found a room in the mine," Mike explained, "but we need to get some lumber and four-by-fours to reinforce the mine entrance. That way, anyone who goes into the mine will be safe."

Pete said, "John, take your pickup truck and go get the council. It is time for them to be here. Mike, you take your other brother and get to Ajo. You know what we need to support the walls and the roof, just about fifteen feet long for both walls. The entrance is about four by four feet at the opening, so we should have about four-by-four feet long to support the walls and roof. Check the price and see if they have what we need. I am sure the council will pay for this after they investigate our findings."

John soon returned, followed by the tribal council members in their van. Watching them approach, Stan said, "Look, Russ, the chiefs are being followed," so I told Stan and Bob to go get a better look at the visitors following the van. They quickly ran to the nearest high ground so they could have an overall view of the valley.

The chiefs got out of their van and, along with their driver and the policeman who was protecting them, approached the shaded area under our break tent. "Pete and Russ," one chief said, "show us what you have uncovered in that mine shaft."

"We are finishing up the necessary shoring so that it will be safe to enter the mine," I replied.

The chief councilman said, "While we wait, tell us what we are going to see."

Pete began, "We noticed that all these rocks are black on top but white on the bottom."

One councilman said, "We all know that. Anyone who grew up in this desert knows that."

Another councilman said, "Look at all those spiders coming this way. What is up? Are we in any danger standing here?"

I said, "Do not worry. You will be okay. Just stay with us and do not run.

When Bob and Stan returned, a councilman asked, "Is that dog playing with that bobcat?" When we explained that they were good friends, the chief councilman asked, "Russ, is that the cat that put the child molester up that cactus next to your house in Ajo?"

I replied, "You are one smart chief," and we all laughed.

Then Stan went over to Pete, put his front paws on Pete's shoulders, and whispered in his ear, "Pancho and his gang are looking down on us right now."

Pete immediately spoke up and said, "The boys have the shoring done, so let us walk over to the mine and take a good look at the two stone boxes in that room."

The chief said, "John did not tell us anything about the boxes."

I replied, "He did not know about the boxes, which look like caskets. We found them after we cleared the rocks away from the tunnel into the mine, and we decided to wait until you all were here to see what is inside."

Pete said, "Okay, Russ, you got us all in this Tarantula Mine, so you do the honors."

The councilmen all agreed, "If there is a curse on these boxes, let it be on the one who opens them."

I said, "I was not thinking about that when I pried the first box open and found this old Spaniard, with his full-body suit of armor covering his bones. He looks like a museum display of an old Spanish conquistador."

Excited, the council members said, "The other casket must be his treasure. Open it now."

So, I took the pry bar and opened the second box, which held a large tarantula nest. Many spiders came out of the box in a wave and proceeded out of the mine, avoiding us but putting a lot of fear into the councilmen.

We could hear something happening outside, so we all walked single file out of the mine. It was Pancho and his gang, and Pancho demanded that we give him the treasure that we had found. I said, "Okay, you can have it all. Just do not hurt any of us. Inside the mine are two boxes waiting for you." Pancho and his gang had guns and had taken down the policeman who had arrived with the council.

Pancho sent his top two men into the mine. Soon we heard them screaming, and they came running out of the mine with a hundred or more tarantulas hanging on them. The two men swatted at the spiders, but the creatures climbed up to their faces and took them down to the ground. I heard Mike exclaim, "Cool!" Pancho saw the spiders forming themselves into a barrier that he and his gang could not escape. Stan and Bob walked up to Pancho, and when Bob let out the most terrifying cat scream that I have ever heard, Pancho shit and peed his pants and dropped his weapons to the ground. All the gang members were covered with tarantulas and scared half to death, so they did what their leader had just done to himself.

We released the policeman and said, "Now you can arrest them."

But he said, "No, they stink too much for the van. I will use the radio and get some policemen on horseback here to herd them to jail like we did for one of these gang members a few weeks ago. By the time they get to jail, their clothes will be dry, and they will always stink like the shits that they are."

The council members were full of questions: "Why did the spiders leave us alone but attack Pancho's gang? Do you have the power to control the dog and that bobcat? We have seen them react to your hand movements and words, and they seem to obey you because they like you. They also seem to have the ability to communicate with you. Are you some sort of wizard or shaman? We like you all very much, because when universities come here, their digs take an exceedingly long time. Why did it not take you long? It has been only three or four months, and already we have a casket of bones and a casket of spiders. We will be calling the university to come here and take over this project, as you have given them a good start on what is out here in this valley."

Chapter 3

We decide

I answered all their questions at once: "No, we are not wizards. All we have done is follow the map. As for the spiders, look at the map and the painting of the spider woman. I am sure that the spiders for whom this valley was named do not want to be disturbed by a bunch of oversexed university students. It might be a good idea to send what was found, including this map, directly to the chair of the department of ancient American history—or someone who is not interested in spending months digging around all these tarantulas in this heat. The suit of armor, bones, and map will tell a good story, and you can limit the use of this land and keep it clean from the trash of some Americans. You can send your young men out here to pick up the brass, which you and your tribe can make some money from and help your homeland prosper. You can trust some of us white men, but not all of us."

As we loaded up our vehicles, I handed the council chief our expense sheet. He said, "You have charged us too little for the service that you have done for the tribe. The lesson that we have learned today is that all men who are honest with us can be trusted friends."

I replied, "Thank you, but June and I are the only white people here. Pete and his family are some of the best, most trustworthy Indians whom I know, but they live here with the rest of your tribe. Chief, please contact me or Pete if you need our help on any future project, and we will come to your aid as needed."

As we prepared for our trip back to our homes, Pete asked, "What is the next project that we can do?"

I answered, "Come to our house on Saturday, and we will have a party away from the cactus wine. We'll have good white man food and beer."

Saturday night, after the party, we all sat around my coffee table with the trunk nearby and started looking for the next step in our quest to find what my uncle was looking for. John said, "Look, this map shows a lost Silver Stairway Mine, but that is not a lost mine. It is about ten miles from our house in Pisin Mo'o, over by the Gunsight town ruins, and it was worked out of silver and lead years ago. Dad, you know, where you found some old guns with your metal detector last year?"

Pete sat up straight and said, "That was just after the Tucson newspaper ran a story about that old Papago who uncovered that stash of old military weapons that the Apache and other tribes hid from the army and the miners. The old Indian said that he did not want to go to war again with anyone."

I spoke up and said, "If this mine is known to everyone around here, why did Uncle Jack have this map and the instructions about where we should start this new quest? I think the council will let us look around for a little while, since we did a good job for them last time."

Pete said, "We need to study this paperwork that Jack left for Russ. You young men go to the library in Ajo and ask for any information about this Silver Stairway Mine and Gunsight that they have in the county's library system. I will call Mike at the university and ask him for any help they can give us."

Then Angel said, "Here is one on Montezuma's Head over there in the Ajo Mountains. This is one of the most photographed mountain peaks in Arizona, and its history is included in many books. Why was this so important to your uncle?"

"I don't know," I answered. "What does it mean that he was also looking around Black Mountain near Ajo?"

Manuel said, "We need to organize these projects and take them one by one."

"Let us take the one near Gunsight next," suggested Pete, "and just keep planning all the rest that seem to be in this neighborhood.

John said, "Here is a map to the Lost Shoemaker or the Lost Soap Makers Mine. Are these the same mine?"

"That mine has already been found," I said. "I made that discovery on my own. Do you remember my trip into the desert after I returned to Ajo? I told you all my story, and you thought that I was hallucinating. We do not need to make that part of our quest, because it was the first step."

Pete said, "We do not need this side trip at all, since we do not want to travel too far from home yet. We need more experience, which we will get on quick projects, since we will never know what is hidden out there until we uncover it. After all, isn't that what we signed up for? This has been fun! Don't forget what we did to those bad boys, whom I hear now love spiders in so many ways."

"As we get better at this, some of our projects will bring in good rewards," I said. "The project involving the lost De Estine Shepherd Mine has a value of more than five million dollars in 1898 gold prices, with 10 to 20 percent finder's fee today. So, let us start slowly and grow up along the way. We can study each case until we come to understand this quest better. Let us do what Manuel has suggested: study the maps, books, and trinkets in this trunk as if each one is a clue that could lead us to discovery."

The earliest recorded history of the Gunsight mine dates from November 1878 when two prospectors came across old silver workings and staked a claim. They named their claim Gunsight because a nearby mountain cut resembled the sight on a rifle. By 1892, the mine was in full operation with eight buildings, a mining camp, and a post office. The original ore from the Gunsight Mine was shipped by wagon to Yuma on the road used by the mines around Ajo for copper, silver, and other metals, and then by sailing ship to Swansea, Wales, for processing.

"We need to get the business going on Montezuma's treasure—or Montezuma's Head—and maybe look at Utah for information on this treasure," I said. As a boy, I had heard about Montezuma's Spanish treasure in the Ajo Mountain Range. Many of the stories were about Montezuma's Head, an impressively tall mountain peak overlooking the Ajo Valley. Following one of my breaks from the navy, I had surveyed the mountain range. I would need to tell the team to watch out and avoid falling into mine shafts. I thought it might be a good idea to find a hole and explore it together. If we asked, maybe the little people would come to our aid, as they had for me in the mine shaft west of Ajo a few months earlier. That might help us solve the myth of the treasure. I was sure that would help other treasure hunters too because their maps were just trash, leading them to harm and even death in the desert.

I then had a second thought: Why hadn't the bottle told me that he could read minds and warn me of these things? I had known for some time that he was able to intrude on my thoughts, but I was always blaming the dog. I thought, *I must ask the bottle a few new questions.* I went into the bedroom where the bottle was kept and asked my first question: "What is your true name?"

The bottle replied, "Why is that important to you now?"

"I asked you a question, and you answered with a question," I said. "Okay, I will play this game with you. I will state my question another way, and I expect a true answer from you. Before your name was the Bishop's Pint, what was your name?"

Then the bottle responded, "Russ, you are one well-informed man. How did you know that I had another name?"

"I read books the old way—not from what I drink, but the drink helps me reason things out," I said.

The bottle said in a loud voice, "Well, then, I will tell you my story, which you probably learned with your first drink from the glass. That little bottle is dropping too many hints to the people who drink from the glass, and I forgot that he could do that. I am *Bacbuc*, which is Hebrew for 'bottle.' The anthem sung before the fleet set sail went like this, 'When Israel went out of bondage,' and all the emblems of the ships bore the proverb 'In vino veritas.' Bacbuc is both the bottle and the priestess of the bottle. I am also called the oracle of the bottle, and the glass is my assigned helper. However, you cannot tell this to the Catholics who are on your team. They might turn on you, and then you would never finish this quest that you took over from your uncle. Another thing for you to know is that the little glass may have already planted that seed deep in their minds, and I don't remember how that fat bishop got me the bottle."

Meanwhile Mike was researching the myth of the lost treasure of Montezuma. His results, taken from a book on Spanish history in the school's library, appeared in his letter to his father: "In 1519, the Spanish conquistador Hernan Cortés arrived on the outskirts of Tenochtitlan, the capital of the mighty Aztec Empire. It has been said that to the Aztec emperor, Montezuma II, Cortés, and his men were regarded not as mortals, but as gods. Cortés himself was said to be the returning Aztec god, Quetzalcoatl. Thus, the Spanish conquistadors were welcomed by Montezuma with pomp and circumstance. Yet eventually these so-called 'gods' betrayed Montezuma and his people, demonstrating to the Aztecs that there was nothing godlike about Cortés and his crew.

"Montezuma's offering of gold to Cortés and his men was done in the hope that the 'gods' would go away. This bribe, however, failed to get rid of the Spanish conquistadors. Instead, it fueled the Spanish greed for gold even further. As a result, Cortés decided to place Montezuma under house arrest. Subsequently, with the help of their Tlaxcalan allies, the conquistadors set up their base in one of the city's temples and began ransacking Tenochtitlan for its treasures. In the following months, many of Tenochtitlan's inhabitants were tortured and killed by Cortés's men in their attempt to obtain even more Aztec treasure. This huge number of precious items eventually came to be known as 'Montezuma's treasure,' and like all good treasure stories, numerous legends have sprung up around this treasure.

"The only thing that is certain about Montezuma's treasure is that it has not been found. Numerous theories have been put forward to suggest the location of its final resting place. For instance, the most popular theory is that the precious objects remain where they were dropped, to the bottom of Lake Texcoco. Numerous treasure hunters have searched the lake, however, but to no avail. Another theory claims that the treasure was retrieved by the Spaniards when they returned to Tenochtitlan, but the ship that was carrying the treasure back to Spain sank in a storm. Perhaps one of the most intriguing theories is that the treasure traveled north, and eventually ended up in Utah."

In his letter to Pete, his father, Mike added, "Arizona is on the path to Utah, so we should start working on the theory that Montezuma's Head is a marker in the route to Utah. And in the Ajo Mountains, there are a lot of nooks and canyons that have never been explored. When do we begin? Dad, there are so many topographical maps of the area on file, made by the USGS in the 1960s. I think I heard that Russ had a lot of experience in the mapping of this area back then. He will be an incredible resource, since he might have been one of the last men to survey these mountains and canyons."

Finally, the quest resumed. Stan, Bob, June, and I were ready to put together the team of everyone who was available for a short trip into the Ajo Mountains. We had our permits, and we needed to follow the rules. We met up with Pete and Angel, along with their two sons who were not at the university. Pete said, "Mike will come on weekends to help. Russ, do you have the permits?" Our little caravan drove south to the park headquarters so that we could sign into the mountain range and set up our base camp, where we could sleep, cook, eat, and shower in the camp shower that Pete had brought with him. I took note of the small portable pot that we had to use, as we had to follow the rules. Bob and Stan were off exploring the area, but the rangers did not know that the bobcat was with us.

I then told Pete and his family that I had come up with a new plan, which was to look for a cave or mine shaft that looked like we could explore the inside. That way, maybe we could find the little people who had rescued me from the mine shaft that I had fallen into the last time I was in the west valley. If we found them, we might be able to get them to help with our quest, especially since they would know everything that was underground. I felt that because of their concern for life and safety, they would like to help us stop the intruders into the underworld.

Pete asked me, "How do we find them—assuming that they are real and not just one of your hallucinations."

I replied, "Pete, have you ever heard stories of miners who said someone was knocking on the walls in the mines of England? That knocking is the little people telling the miners that they are not alone. So, I think that once we are underground, we start knocking on the walls to let them know that they are not alone. We can also speak to them and tell them who we are and why we are in their underground world."

Pete said, "Okay, we'll start this search one canyon at a time in the morning. Now we should settle into our tents and sleep the night away, as we prepare our minds for this new quest."

The next morning, we were awakened by the park ranger and the caretaker of the camping area, who came around every Tuesday morning to pick up the trash and any litter in the camping area. The ranger warned us that the caretaker would report any trash blowing around the camp, so we should be mindful and pick up any trash that we dropped or noticed blowing around.

When I said, "I am glad that we don't have to cut the grass," the ranger laughed and got into his truck. Then the caretaker dumped the trash barrels into the back of his truck, waved goodbye, and drove out of the camping area."

We were ready to start exploring the Ajo Mountain Range, and the wonderful smell of the breakfast that Angel was cooking got everyone out of bed. Pete said, "Look, Mike is here."

As I walked up to Mike, he said, "The council is having trouble in Spider Valley with the university. The professors are going crazy over the ghost of a woman walking in and out of the mine tunnel. He called me because he could not find you or Dad. You did tell him to get you if they needed you and Dad."

Stan said, "Oh no, it must be the spiders. I thought that I understood them when we were talking 'mind to mind,' but I must have missed something in the translation."

Then Pete said, "You made a mistake? Stan, this is unbelievable coming from you. You have been so good with us."

I asked, "Mike, what did the council say?" He told me that they claimed to have seen a woman who looked like she was wearing spiders. Since they could see through her, they thought she was a ghost.

Pete asked, "What are we to do, Russ?"

"Today we do a walk through the first canyon, and then we sleep tonight," I replied. "Tomorrow we just may have the answer to the council's problem. It should not take us long, but if you do not like female ghosts, Pete, you can stay here with the women. I also think that Mike and I can resolve this problem, and then he can return to the university. This is not a weekend, so he needs to get back to his studies."

As we started our walk, we took in the elegance of the plants, lizards, snakes, spiders, and scorpions in the first canyon. We took notes on what we were seeing so that we would remember to remain alert for these little monsters, as we did not know what was ahead of us on this project. Then, after eating our sack lunches, we continued down the other side of the canyon and back to the camping area, where we dumped our trash from lunch in the trash can and carefully replaced the lid. We did not find any mines or caves on our first trip through that canyon. After cleaning ourselves up, we had our supper and then sat around talking about the Spider Valley problem.

June asked, "Russ, what do you think the problem is?"

I replied, "Let us all take a drink from the bottle and go to bed. When we get up in the morning, we may find the answer around the breakfast table. I will get the bottle and the glass, and we will each have a drink. Stan will go with Mike and me on the trip back to Spider Valley." So, we drank and went to bed to sleep and dream. Boy, did I have a dream! The oracle of the bottle came through with this problem, and then I knew that we had a solution to the ghost in Spider Valley.

When morning came, the team found me walking around the camp. I was smiling and laughing, and June asked, "Russ, what is going on?"

Mike said, "June, I guess that you did not have the same dream that Russ and I had last night. I was not sure, but after seeing Russ this morning, I know that he and I had the same dream. We know the answer to the Spider Valley ghost."

After breakfast, Mike got in his car, and Stan and I got in mine. We were off to solve the ghost problem, as we knew what to do. Stan said, "I knew there was something I did not understand from those spiders. How did you work it out?"

I replied, "I had a visitor during the night. Do you remember the big spiders we saw in the canyon yesterday? One came to visit last night and told me what we did wrong that day in Spider Valley. All that we have to do is convince the professor that she is a crazy woman who should take a long vacation away from the valley." When Stan asked how I was going to do that, I said, "I am not going to do it—you are. Just talk to her, and then she will be ready to go to a hospital. Then I will work with the council to get the conquistador back into the mine with the two stone coffins and cover up the mine like it was before we came into the valley."

What we had thought was a mine was a tomb for the dead conquistador and his bride, the spider woman. It is good to know the stories of the Southwest and some of Mexico. Spider women myths are common, but this one is not a myth. The council would get the two coffins back with the conquistador and place them back in the tomb, where they had been before we disturbed them. You just cannot mess with Indian myths and legends because they will always get you in the end.

As we arrived in the valley, the council was waiting for us. "What are we going to do about this problem?" they asked. "The professor is in a completely crazy fit again, and more of her student workers are leaving every day. This ghost is driving us all crazy, and we just don't know what to do."

I said, "We are here to help you. Where is the professor right now?" The chief told me that she was in the big tent in front of the mine, so I said to Stan, "Come with me. We are going to visit with the lady in the tent."

As we walked to the tent, Stan asked, "What am I to do?"

"First, we should make her feel better," I replied. "If you will lick her hand, she should relax. I will tell her that I am here to help her and that I found the dig. Then Mike will call me, and I will go into the tomb. That's when you can start your story with her."

Stan asked, "What story?"

I said, "Anything that comes into your mind, such as how you talk to the spiders." Well, we did have a quick visit, and she did relax. Then Mike called to me, and I went into the tomb.

Suddenly the professor came out of the tent screaming and told the council that she quit. She said that she was on her way to a hospital because this project had broken her mind, and she was going to get some help with her illness. "I will notify the university," she yelled, "that this project will drive anyone who works on it crazy, with all the spiders and other strange things." When I asked if she needed someone to drive her back to Tucson, she replied, "I can drive my car. I must just be crazy."

The chief said, "The policeman will follow you back to Tucson, just to make sure you make it home safely."

After she left, the chief asked how I persuaded her to go to the hospital for help. I said, "You know that you are smart," and then I whispered, "but I am a wizard." Then I said, "The Indian myth about the spider woman and the conquistador is that they were man and wife, and this mine is actually their tomb. You need to get the conquistador's bones back into the casket, and then hide the tomb and forbid entry to this sacred valley. Do not allow any digs and keep a policeman at every entry into the canyon so that the god in the tomb will not upset the spider woman."

The chief said, "This will take some time, but we will go to Washington, DC, and get it done. Russ, thank you again for your honesty. I am sure that things will now become stable here in Spider Valley."

Mike and I said our goodbyes, and he started his trip back to the university. Stan and I got on the road back to the Ajo Mountains and our new project feeling great. Stan said, "That professor was just a little bit crazy until I told her that I could talk to the spiders for her." I could not hold back my laughter.

We arrived back at the Ajo Mountains just in time to eat supper and report to the team about how we had handled the spider problem in just one day. As we all sat around the table, Pete asked, "What did you do, Russ? One of your old navy tricks?"

I said, "No, we used the bottle and let it do its job. Right, Stan?"

Stan said, "I just told the professor that I could talk to the spiders for her, and Russ talked to the council. The professor went completely out of her mind and drove herself to get medical help. Russ told the council that they should shut down the dig, as no one would work on a site where a ghost walked around dressed in spiders. He explained to them that the mine was actually a tomb for a royal god of the Aztecs, the spider woman, who is known in myth and legend to be entombed with a loyal servant and protector."

Then I said, "The tribal council is moving to secure the valley and get the caskets and bones returned to the tomb. Then they will seal the tomb and protect it from treasure seekers, since we should not be responsible for danger and fear of the unknown. If the federal government gets involved, it will be on them. We need some rest, and then let us start where you left off in the morning."

Pete said, "Wait, Russ, I have a report on what we did today without you. My boys and I walked the first canyon at a different level than yesterday, so that we could look up and down to the canyon bottom, and we found more spiders and small wildlife. Bob was with us, but she disappeared for a while. We do not know where she went, but after she returned, she started making a bit of a fuss about something. So, we stopped and marked the spot where we had lost sight of her. Then we returned here to the camp to wait for you and Stan. I think we should start at the place we marked in the morning."

I asked, "What did you feel when Bob returned to you?"

Pete said, "I felt pressure. I was unable to think about anything, but the bobcat was at the point of the pressure in my mind."

Then Manuel and John said, almost at the same time, "All we felt, and thought was that Bob was trying to tell us something."

"It is time again to consult the bottle," I said, "so that we can understand Bob and our surroundings." So, I got the bottle and glass, and we all had another drink. This time we brought Stan and Bob into the drink with us, and all the team except Mike. Then we were ready for some rest and sleep.

During the night, I was awakened by noise outside my sleeping tent, so I went outside to see what was making the sound. I saw several small people, the Knockers from underground, with a message for me. They said that they had met my friend Bob when she fell into a hole or vent for the underground. The bobcat had asked them for help and told them my story from the old shoemaker mine. The Knockers said they were well versed in how I had helped one of their old enemies, the spider woman, on the previous day. They said they knew I wanted to keep the underground safe for everyone, so they would help me and my friends and family. They also could hardly wait to hear the dog talk.

When I mentioned that I had not known that Bob could talk, they said, "No talk. Just thoughts."

Then Stan and Bob joined us, and Stan said, "So you are the Knockers that Russ has told us about. I am Stan, the dog that you would like to meet and hear talk. How can I be of service to you, friends of Russ?"

The head spokesman of the Knockers said, "Thank you, Stan. We can see you and hear you speak, but we also hear your thoughts, just like we hear Bob's. We come out into this upper world only when the sun is on the other side of the planet, so we have contact only with those with whom we want to be involved, such as you and your party of friends. We need to have this visit known by all of you at this place now. Could you call them all?"

Stan said, "I like to do that. I guess it is a dog thing." Then he ran from tent to tent, calling everyone to come to the meeting immediately. As we all assembled around the camp table, there was some surprise about the group of little people. Everyone wondered what was going on.

The head Knocker called us to order and started our meeting, this time in the dark. He said, "We will help with your quest if you follow a few restrictions. First, do not tell anyone about us in the underworld. Second, if you have trash with you in the underworld, carry it out when you leave. And third, you must use our system for your sanitation needs. We will direct you to those stations, as we have many of them. Does everyone agree to these rules?"

I asked, "Team, do you all agree? Each person must answer individually, as I cannot make a statement for all of us without your response."

Pete said, "Yes, I agree," and Angel followed with "I will." Manuel and John each said that they would also follow the rules. Then Manuel asked, "What about Mike? He is not here to take this step. Will he be able to come and help us on his school breaks?"

The Knockers' head man said, "Your Mike will take this step when he is with us."

June and I both said that we also agreed with the rules.

Then the head Knocker said, "We will start when the sun is in the mountains. Bob will lead you to the hole he fell into, so that we can direct you to a larger entrance to the underworld."

We went back to our tents and rested until the sun came up, when we were awakened by the smell of the bacon and eggs that June and Angel were frying for breakfast. The smell of bacon is a stimulating thing for all of us humans—cats and dogs, too. We ate our meal in silence and then were in a hurry to get to the spot that Bob had found. The women said that they would like to go to Lukeville, Arizona, for more supplies for the team. They also wanted to get some cakes, candy bars, and other food that the little people might want.

I said, "Have a fun day, and please keep out of Mexico."

Pete added, "No beer or wine until this project is over."

June replied, "You guys take the fun out of everything."

Bob was acting a bit strange as we set out, and we heard her make an unusual sound. Then she said, "Come on, team. Follow me."

Stan said, "Oh boy, a female cat that can talk now. What next?"

As we started to hike into the canyon, we had to ask Bob to slow down a bit, as we did not want to lose her. She turned around and waited for us poor humans to catch up. When we were all together again, Bob said, "Sorry, I just got carried away with this new me." Then we were able to hear her mind, which was new to us. We all had changed during the quest, and we were able to hear the birds, lizards, snakes, rats, and mice—all the living things in the desert. We were now able to live a better life in the desert, knowing what was underfoot so that we could watch out for ourselves, other people, and all the little critters. Now, that is a good feeling, and maybe we will make a difference on this planet called Earth.

As we continued our hike into the canyon, we heard Bob say, "We are here now, and I think we should rest from the heat of this sun while we wait for the Knockers."

After a short wait, the head Knocker poked his head out of the hole and said, "I see that your minds are active. Follow my thoughts, and I will be waiting at a good entrance to the underworld."

I said, "Look, we have been here before, during out preliminary search of this canyon. Look at this photo on my camera. Why did we not see this hole then?"

Suddenly a voice came out of the hole, saying, "You were not in tune with the earth, so you just missed the tunnel."

We turned around and entered a cave in the Ajo mountain range. Walking into a great room, we saw many Knockers sitting in rows before a group of older Knockers that looked like a Council of Leadership.

The largest Knocker said, "I am the one chosen to lead these Knockers in their journey through the underworld. You were told that we have rules, but you have not sworn to follow all the rules. There is one more that you need to agree with now. If any of us discovers Aztec treasure, it shall belong to the Knockers in payment for the way they treated us in the past. However, you will receive 10 percent of what any of us finds. Do you all agree?"

I said, "That is agreeable to me." Turning to Pete, John, and Manuel, I asked, "What do you three say to this rule?"

Pete said, "I am okay with the rule," and John and Manuel agreed with their father.

It occurred to me that June, Angel, and Mike would also agree. Then, in my mind, I heard the Knocker chief say, *"They have already agreed. That is how things work now, but do you wish to verify it with your lady, June? She would like to tell you something. Just call out to her in your thoughts, and you will be able to hear her and Angel in the upper world."*

So, I did just that, and I heard June like we were talking on a phone. I told her that I loved her, and I asked what she and Angel were doing. She said, "We are here in camp, waiting for you loved ones to return to us. Just where are you and Pete and the boys right now?"

I answered that we were somewhere in the underworld thinking about her, and that we would try to get back to the camp that night, although I was not sure when the council meeting would end. Then I turned to the Knocker chief and asked, "When will we start this search for Montezuma's treasure, and can our ladies come with us, as they will be a good help to all of us?"

The Knocker chief said, "You men are here to help us, so we will help you. The mine in the Gunsight mountain range is not a place for you to go. The water is bad, and it destroys the mind. We see this in your minds, and you know what this problem is. Tell us why the water is so bad for all the life that drinks from the wells."

I said, "Men dug in this mine for silver, lead, arsenic, and other metals. I think that lead poisons the brain of anyone who uses it either inside or outside their body. Arsenic poisons slowly and in small doses can cause years of physical suffering before death finally occurs. As for the other metals, I do not know. Water from the mine, which could be full of such minerals, would present a great hazard, but it can be filtered for use if you have what you need for the process. I think we can put behind us any exploration of the Silver Stairway Lost Mine at Gunsight."

Then I turned to Pete and said, "I think I heard one of your boys say that the tribal council was going to put a casino in that area close to Why. Meanwhile, let us continue with this meeting and search for the Aztec treasure."

We told the Knockers what Mike had found in the university library— the recorded searches for this treasure—that led us to believe that it was in this mountain range, perhaps in a cave in the area. We thought that the Knockers might know whether that was true.

The chief of the Knockers said, "Throughout history, my people have known of this story. They have been tracking the treasure for many rotations of the earth and sun, keeping a record of their searches on the walls of this cave. Let me take you there." As we all walked through the cave, it occurred to me that many years had passed since Cortes's arrival in Mexico, so that would be an awfully long record. As we arrived at the point of the cave to which the chief had led us, he said, "Here, look at the writings on the wall. This is where we are today." Looking at the wall, we saw a fresh painting of five tall men with two tall women, a dog, a bobcat, and what looked like spiders.

After looking at the paintings and taking photos for a while, we were getting tired. I said to the chief, "We must return to the surface to study the photographs that we have taken of the wall, at least the short area that we have been in. We also need some rest, but we will return soon."

As we started back, Bob said, "I hope the women took care of my sons while we were away."

When Pete asked how long we had been down there, I said, "I don't know, but we will find out when we get to the surface."

We emerged from the cave into the dark of night, and we had to hike down the canyon very carefully as our flashlights were getting dim. As we approached base camp, we did not see any activity, and Stan and Bob ran ahead to check the area around the tents. The vehicles were there, but the women were not visible to us. We were worried that something had gone wrong, so Pete and I both cried out with our new gift of thought, ready to communicate with the whole team.

The first team member to answer was Mike, who was in Tucson. "How did you call me?" he asked. "This seems strange to me. Am I dreaming? What is going on, Dad?"

Pete answered, "We are at base camp now. Have you heard from your mother or June today?"

Mike said, "No, but why are you asking me? You all went into the cave a week ago. Are you telling me that you are just now getting back to base camp? And is Mom not there?"

"Well," I said, "now we know how long we were in the cave."

Then we saw Stan and Bob running back toward us, each carrying a baby bobcat that was not enjoying the trip. Stan said, "The women are asleep. Bob wanted her babies, so we brought them with us so that you would know everything is okay in the camp."

June and Angel came out of their tents and asked, "What is going on out here?"

I said, "We did not know how long we had been gone. We thought it was only one day."

"One day is equal to a week underground. We must have crossed into another time zone down there," said Pete.

I then shared my theory that the Knockers were the Chichimecs from the early days of the Aztec empire: "When they told me their story when I was in the hole of the Shoemaker Lost Mine, it was like it had all happened yesterday. Their race must be incredibly old. We need to protect them and keep their existence secret so that they will remain safe. In the process, we might experience more time travel, so we must always keep track of where we are while in the underworld. Make marks, paint on the walls, tunnels, and rocks—anything that will help us find our way out of the underworld. Also, we may meet up with the Zotz, the bat god of caves."

Pete said, "If we meet up with Zotz, we might also meet other Aztec gods. We must always be alert and on guard, watching our thoughts at all times in that new time zone."

Later that night, I rose from my camp bed and went outside our tent. While I was there, the park ranger showed up with two young ladies, whom he introduced as Miss White and Miss Wong. "These two ladies will be your neighbors for a few days," he said. "They have been told the rules of this campground, and they won't interfere with your camp or what you are doing here."

I felt it strange that the ranger was setting up the ladies' campsite and making sure that I knew their names. Surely there was more to that situation than the ranger had shared with us. Was he perhaps warning us to be on guard around them? I returned to my bed and told everyone "Good night," and the team all did the same, sounding off with their names. Then there came a faint sound from Miss White and Miss Wong, adding to the good night message. My first thought when I heard them was that they wanted to join our group. I turned to June and said, "This is strange," but she just told me to go to sleep.

The next morning, we got up and looked around the camp, ready to pick up trash and put it in the cans. Pete asked, "What was that thing I heard you thinking about last night? It sounds like we need to do our talking with our minds instead of our mouths."

I then said what I had been thinking all night: "I believe that the two women are spies from the university. Can you get in touch with Mike with your new abilities?"

Pete thought, *"It worked in the cave for you, so I will give it a try. What are we going to tell the team?"*

Then a thought entered both of our minds at once: *"We already know. Even the dog and cats know. Bob has never had any experience with a spy, the kittens are upset and afraid, and Stan thinks that spies are everywhere."*

Just then I heard Angel call, "You all can come to breakfast now."

I called back, "Okay, we are on our way." Then it occurred to me that maybe we could play them a bit. "Pete, can you and Angel give us a prayer song with a drum and ask the boys to dance before breakfast? And when we start to eat, let us all shout 'Amen!' loudly enough so that we will be heard."

Everyone agreed, and one person even said, "Yes, it will be fun. Even a Catholic can have fun."

As Pete and I were getting our backpacks together, we both pulled out empty wine bottles, so I asked to refill them from the big bottle in the trunk of the car.

"Russ, our bottles are also empty. Can we fill them up too?" asked Angel.

"Yes, and have a good day," I said. "Stay off the roads."

Pete said, "Time is running short. We need to get there soon to look at the rest of the work. You boys walk the campgrounds, and if you find any of our friends, tell them hello."

"Will do, Dad," said John.

As we hiked into the canyon, I noticed that the two women got in their car and drove away in a hurry. I said to Pete, "I wonder where they are going." When we were halfway into the canyon, we heard a helicopter overhead, circling back and forth between us and our destination, so we just turned around. On our hike back, we saw the helicopter fly back toward the park headquarters. Just as we got back to camp, the two women drove back into the campground.

I nudged Pete's mind: *"I guess they saw that we were looking up at them following us by air. The park ranger told us that they would not bother us on our project."*

After we sat around our camp table enjoying a small drink from our bottles of wine, we got up and went into our tents. Then I said, "Let us go into Lukeville and have a good meal and a beer or two. June, you are the

55

designated driver, so no beer for you on this trip." We all got into John's new van and drove out of the camp, leaving Stan on guard with Bob and the kittens. But first we asked Stan and Bob not to resort to violence when the two ladies looked through our camp.

When we returned, Stan came running. Through his thoughts, we learned that those two spies did go through our tents. *"They took two bottles of wine with them, and that is the only thing that I saw them do, those bitches. It took a lot to keep Bob from killing them when she saw them reach down to pet her kittens. She did that thing that makes men climb a cactus or shit themselves. I heard a fart when they ran out of the tent. They rushed to their tent screaming all the way, and then they threw their pants and things on the ground. I checked them out and it was just piss. Then I heard them laughing and talking about the wine and how good it tasted. They said that now they had something that made them smarter than the professor. Look at this, Russ. I took the full bottle out of their tent. Do you think we could fill it with something special so that they can take it back with them to the university?"*

"Fill it with what?" asked Pete.

Then I said, "John, with all that beer you drank, do you think that you could fill the bottle with your piss?"

"I can try," John replied, "but I think Stan should put some of his in the bottle too. That would be a good thing for the university lab to investigate."

Pete was thinking, *"Just what is this little job that you sent my son on? Is it dangerous?"*

I answered, *"I sent him around the campground to collect all the spiders that were in the mine shaft, to visit when we come back into camp. I will instruct the spiders in what we need them to do for the team."*

We continued our hike in the second canyon, surveying the plant life and writing a report that could be taken when all the team was away from the camp. When we returned to camp around noon, the team's family was sitting in the shade and talking about the beauty of the desert plants and wildlife. It seemed like our plan would work on the two female spies.

I said, "I think the lady professor will have company in the hospital."

Stan asked, "What do I do?"

"Just watch," I replied.

After we gave the message to the spiders in our circle, the number of spiders was increasing to help keep the spider woman safe from any more intrusions into her tomb. It was nice to have so much help and support.

Pete asked, "What is our part in this party? What can we all do to make this happen?"

"Just perform the dance and prayer song with the drum playing," I said. "I am sure this will bring the two ladies out to watch us. Then spider woman will make her appearance, performing her moves to the rhythm of the drum. After that, I do believe the two spies will just scream, get in their car, and rush to the ranger station for help getting to the hospital."

Pete said, "So that is what you did in the navy? You are a spook. Okay, Sir Spook, why did we waste hours filling out all those plant and wildlife reports?"

I replied, "When the police and the FBI do their investigation, we must have all the survey reports on hand for the search warrant. That way our reason for being here will appear to match what is on our permit from the Park Service. One plus one equals two—or the truth. Bob will have to take her kittens out into the canyon until the university has finished harassing me and the team because of what I did in Spider Valley to keep them out of the tribal lands."

Bob, with her kittens, walked up to the table and said, "We will not be too far away."

Stan said, "I will keep watch for you and the kittens."

When the sun was setting in the west, we started our party, complete with drumming, singing, and dancing. Miss White and Miss Wong emerged from their tent to listen and watch. When Pete paused his song, the spiders did their part, just about a yard apart, and the spider woman stood up and moved to the drum. Miss White screamed and pointed at the tall spider woman, and then Miss Wong did the same thing. They both ran to their car and drove away toward the park office in one high-speed trip down the road.

Watching them drive away, I said, "We should be able to return to our work in a few days." After thanking our friends for their help, we decided to go to bed.

Early the next morning, the FBI arrived by helicopter and the park rangers by car with sirens blasting. As we emerged from our tents, an FBI agent said, in a rather hostile manner, "Come over to the camp table and put your hands on your heads. You are all under arrest."

I asked, "Why? What did we do, who has filed a complaint, and why are you all here? May we see the search warrants?"

One of the park rangers said, "You are on National Park property, and you were warned. The request that you submitted was for permission to survey the Ajo Mountain Range for plants and wildlife. Also, I told you not to interfere with the two female park visitors."

I then said to my team, "Don't answer any questions until they honor our right to have an attorney present." We watched them rip apart our tents and vehicles, with help from the drug dog they had brought with them. When they were finished, I asked, "What has been found? Anything? Our report on our survey is in the unlocked trunk in my tent—or have you destroyed everything in the tent?"

Stan was getting a little mad with the police dog. I could tell that he was in direct contact with that dog, and he started broadcasting what was in the dog's mind, which was good information. The police dog got up from where his handler had left him. The officer was getting mad, as his canine partner was not paying attention to him. It seemed that Stan had the upper hand with the police dog.

Then I got a jolt from Pete, who said, "Stan has done his job and changed the drug dog's mind. What are you going to do, Sir Spook?"

I said to the FBI agent, "Thank you for answering my questions. The university does not like me, because I can talk to the tribal council about their myths and legends without charging them by pilfering the artifacts of their people for months, as the university does. Why do you want to be their lackey by harassing me and my team? You need to talk to those two university spies about this hoax of an investigation. Ask them how they got drunk on a bottle of cactus wine. What reason do they have for interfering in our work with the tribal chiefs? What were the lab results of the bottle they had? If you do not know, ask that police dog who is over there with my dog, Stan."

The agent yelled at his pilot, "Get on the radio and get me a CSI out here ASAP. Then get in the air, pick him up in Tucson, and bring him here. Now!" The helicopter was soon in the air.

Then the agent turned to the police dog handler and asked, "What is wrong with your dog?"

"I don't know," the handler replied. "The other dog just looked at him, and now they're friends and I have no control over him. He will not obey me."

The distance between Tucson and the Ajo Mountain Range was about 136 miles by air, so the CSI would be arriving in two to three hours. Meanwhile, I asked if Angel would cook us some breakfast. With a smile on his face, the FBI agent chimed in, "And some for the FBI too?"

Everyone was wondering what Sir Spook had done to the FBI, so I explained, "I triggered his mind to become an investigator for a change."

The FBI agent walked over to the other agent and a park ranger and said, "Go to a phone and get a background on Russ Philips of Ajo, Arizona."

While we waited to get our freedom back, we all sat down to an incredibly good breakfast.

The FBI agent in charge said, "I don't think it will take long to find out all about you, and I expect that I will be surprised at your background. Look, the park ranger is back already. I wonder what they found out."

The ranger came over to the table and said, "Mr. Philips, I apologize for my behavior and doubting your story."

The FBI agent asked, "What is going on? Where is the background report?"

His partner said, "Here it is, boss," and handed him a fax of my record.

The lead agent said, "I was right—I am surprised." Turning to his team, he said, "Okay, put this place back in the order it was in before our search."

Soon the helicopter returned with the CSI, who was eager to get to work. So, the lead FBI agent said, "I want that tent checked for fingerprints. Then print all these people and compare them."

The CSI replied, "Okay, but can I get the people first? That dog looks like he wants his prints taken too."

"Okay, and get that big spider as well," said the FBI agent.

The CSI started to stomp on the spider, but I stepped in and said, "Don't hurt the spider. He is a friendly one. Look around and you might see all of the spiders in this campground."

Heeding my warning, the CSI said, "It is no wonder that those two women went crazy out here."

Then they all cried out, "Keep the spider woman away from us. This park must be haunted. I don't want to be here too long, so let us get the print collection going."

After our prints were taken and the tent was checked for prints, the CSI said, "None of these prints belong to these nice people."

Then the lead FBI agent said, "Mr. Philips, what tent did you say was searched by others?"

Running over to the tent that June and I were using, Stan barked. I said, "Where Stan is standing."

Seeing that he needed to do more prints, the CSI picked up his kit, walked inside my tent, and got to work again. It did not take long, as the first thing he printed was the file chest that contained our records. Finding a print that did not match anyone in our group, he called out, "I've got it. You can now take me back to Tucson and my family." He then walked over to the camp table, checked the prints from the first tent, and said, "Here, Mr. FBI man. These are the prints from Mr. Philips's tent, and they match. Can I go home now?"

I asked, "What was the message from your FBI?"

He said, "Dammit, you already know, don't you? The message said, 'Let Mr. Philips do his job! And leave him and his party alone.'"

I smiled and said, "We might work together someday."

As the FBI boarded the helicopter, and the police and park rangers got into their cars, I reminded the dog handler not to forget his dog. "You will find that he is a better dog after this experience today," I said. "He will follow and answer to you. All you must do is talk to him each day and on every assignment. Maybe you could give him another name, and he will tell you whether it is a good name for him. It will be like he is naming himself. You must trust his decision on his name, as it would be an insult if you don't, and then you would lose him."

Pete said, "All I know now is that you have contacts in DC and that you are a spook. Wonderful! Does this make us targets also?"

"Have you been hurt standing with me and June?" I asked. "Are we friends? Have you checked your bank account lately? Did you know that every member of this team has an account at your bank?"

Pete answered, "No, I didn't know about the bank accounts, nor have I been hurt standing with you and June."

I said, "Tomorrow morning we will all go to the bank in Ajo and check on our accounts."

"What about Mike?" asked Angel.

"Why don't you ask him?" I spoke. "I believe that is him driving up the road." As Mike arrived, we all stood up and clapped to welcome back our prize student. I asked, "Mike, why are you back with us this early? The semester is not over yet."

He said, "I was put out by the regents, who said they did not need my type in their university."

"I guess I must have hit the ball a little too far," I said. "I am sorry, Mike, and I will do my best to clear up this little problem when we get into Ajo to check our bank accounts. Then we will all go to our house so that I can make a phone call without that stranger listening in."

Mike asked his father, "Dad, what is going on here?"

Pete said, "Mike, don't worry. Russ will get things straightened out. He has more power than I ever imagined. One call is all it takes." Then Mike and Pete took a walk to talk with each other.

When Manuel asked, "Can a hungry boy get some food?" both June and Angel got up and started on supper. I asked Stan to get Bob and the kittens and bring them home, and he said, "Along with the bottle and the glass?" I agreed, and he ran toward the canyon to find his friend and her kittens. I said, "I don't think Bob and her children will need to hide when we get questioned again, if ever."

Pete and Mike soon returned to camp, as did Stan, Bob, and her kittens. Then we all sat down for a good meal, and it was off to bed to rest for a busy day in Ajo.

At sunrise, we ate a quick breakfast and then were off to Ajo to do some banking. We parked around the plaza next to the company store, walked up to the stoplight, and crossed the street to the bank. "This is the coldest bank in Ajo," I said, and Pete added, "Yes, and the only bank."

When Pete and Angel Garcia walked up to the bank teller and asked to see their balance, she asked for their account number. Pete looked at me with a puzzled expression, and June said to the three young men, "Russ to the rescue again."

I asked to see the bank manager, who came out of his office and asked, "What is the problem, sir?"

I said, "Here are the account numbers for Pete, Angel, Mike, John, and Manuel Garcia. Please help them open their accounts now. These two account numbers are for Russ and June Philips. We would appreciate quick service, as we have other important business to take care of today so that we can get back to work."

The manager looked at the numbers and told the teller that they were listed in the vault as accounts without names. "Please help them," he instructed the teller. "Check their balances, and issue them bank cards. Then take their photos, as we do for all of our customer accounts."

Starting with Angel, the young teller said, "Oh my, you have a great deal of money." When Angel asked how much money, the teller said, "Twenty thousand dollars." Then she said, "Looking at the Garcia family accounts, I see that you each have that same amount—twenty thousand dollars. That is a hundred thousand for a family of five in Ajo, Arizona. Let me take your pictures so that you will have a photo ID card for your cash needs. Would you each like debit and credit cards too?"

Pete looked at me, but I said, "How you spend your money is up to you. I know that your mine retirement pay is not much, but remember that you are working with me, and I will always support all of you."

Manuel spoke up and asked, "Even the cats and dog?"

"Yes, Manuel, every one of us," I replied.

The teller asked, "Do you have a job for me?"

I said, "You have a job here at this bank, and you will be taking care of our money. I will see that you get a pay raise for the work you are doing. Where is the manager? I need to talk to him right now."

The manager poked his head out of his office and asked, "What is the problem now?"

I said, "I need this young teller to take care of all our accounts. That should be all that she does, and you need to pay her more. What do you pay her now?"

He said, "She gets four hundred dollars a month and not a penny more."

I looked him in the eye and asked, "How much do we trust you to take care of our money? The young lady will show you the total amount in our seven accounts. Then you will double her salary and hire a replacement, so that she can do her job as our account's manager. Otherwise, we will remove our money from your bank. Also, it might be a good idea for you to spend less time in your office. What is your answer? Do we stay with your bank or move our accounts to Tucson and take our accounts manager with us?"

Then I turned to the young lady and asked, "Can you move today?"

"Yes, for a better job," she replied.

I said, "Team, we are almost ready, but first the bank manager needs to do one more thing for us. Okay, Mr. Bank Manager, we will take all our money in cashier's checks now."

He answered, "I can't do this alone. Jill, will you help me since they are your accounts?"

"That will be okay, Jill," I said. "When you finish, bring the checks, and John will take you to your house to help you pack what you will be needing. Then you will come to our house tonight, so that we all can leave for Tucson in the morning."

Turning to the rest of our team, I said, "Let us get home and make the call to straighten out the problems with Mike's education. And Jill, we will talk about your job when you arrive at our home."

With that, Jill went to work for the last time in the bank in Ajo.

When we turned into our driveway, June exclaimed, "We are home!"

Once inside the house, I grabbed the phone and called the number that I used when I needed outside help. First the phone number, followed by the special personal number that indicates that I need help. A voice said, "Hello, Russ. What do you need?" I described the problems that I was having with the university on the reservation.

Then I reported that Mike had been unenrolled from his classes because the regents had claimed that they did not need his type in their university. I said, "I need the two FBI agents to meet with the Garcia's at the university administration offices at two o'clock this afternoon, so that they can set everything right for Mike, who is a loyal team member. You can tell these agents that I was right—we are working on the same case."

When my call was over, I went into the kitchen to tell Mike and his parents that they had a two o'clock appointment with those nice FBI agents, Davis, and Samson, and that they would be meeting with the university administration. "Please let Agent Davis talk first," I said, "and then I think that things will get better for Mike—and any other Native American. Just remember what your report said. If I know Davis, he will put them in their place and scare them."

Acting a little strange, Jill said, "I don't understand what you and your team do. Will I get in any trouble working with this team?"

"You will be safe," I replied, "once you are listed as a member of the team. June, will you add Jill to the team so that she can get her pay and benefits?

June said, "Jill, please come with me into the living room. We need to fill out a document and take a photo for your new ID."

Jill followed June into the living room, and we heard June ask, "What is your full name?" Jill answered, "Jill Anderson."

Then Pete asked, "What about our benefits and ID cards?"

"June will give them to you when we are finished here," I said.

John asked, "Why do we need Jill anyway?"

"We need someone to take care of our bank accounts," I replied, "and we need to trust her. Jill is a hardworking girl, and I like her. We need to add her to our team, give her the whole story, and then give her the same drink that you all had yourselves. I think that June has completed the short form, and the complete team will be in the kitchen, including Stan, Bob, and the kittens. I am glad this house has a large table with eight chairs."

Then I said, "Okay, team, it is time to meet and talk about adding Jill to our team." We each took a chair at the table, and I put the bottle and glass on the table. "This meeting is now called to order. Jill, the team members want to ask you a few questions, and you will need to answer every question. John will go first."

John asked, "What talents will you bring to this team, given that you know nothing about what we do?"

"I have a master's degree in bank management from the university," said Jill, "and I will be taking care of your bank accounts."

Then I asked the team, "Any more questions?"

"I think her answer to John is enough," said June. "Russ, do you have anything to say?"

I said, "Jill, we all came together as a team, and we have all agreed to our quest. Now I want you to meet the team, starting with Stan, the dog.

Bob and her kittens, who are about a year old, are bobcats and amazingly important to our team. Stan and Bob, say hello to Jill."

Stan said, "Hello, I am Stan."

Then Bob said, "Hi, Jill. I am Bob, and these are my children, Bobby and Robby."

Jill looked surprised that the dog and cat could talk, and we were all surprised that the kittens had names. I said, "Bob, you named the kittens? What brought this on?" She replied that everyone needs a name, and I said, "That is wonderful."

Then I again turned my attention to Jill. "You can see that Stan and Bob have special traits not found in other dogs and cats. Now, this bottle and glass are also part of our team. The bottle contains water, and anyone who drinks from the bottle and glass gains the ability to do amazing things. It will uplift you, stimulate your mind, and enrich your ongoing educational life. Are you ready to drink of the bottle and glass?"

John said, "Don't worry, Jill. We will all drink from the bottle to demonstrate that its water will not harm you in any way."

Then I poured a glass for myself and said, "The bottle holds just half a pint. Watch as I go around the table and give each team member a glass of water from it. I will drink mine first and then give a glass each to June, Angel, Pete, Mike, John, and Manuel."

Then Bob jumped onto the table and made her request known. With one lick, she drank her glass, but then she would not get off the table. As her kittens came up to me, I looked at the team members. They all just smiled and nodded, so I poured two more glasses of the water of life for Bobby and Robby, who thus became team members.

Then I walked up to Jill, who agreed to drink from the glass. When she noticed that the bottle was still full, I said, "I have had this bottle for years, and it has never been emptied. Well, what did it taste like?"

Jill said, "Well, it tastes like water."

Turning to June, I asked, "Can we have a meal—or at least some food?"

Stan replied, "Make it good for our new team members, but please also make it good for all of us."

Pete and his family were ready to go to their home on the reservation. He said, "Russ, you have a full house now, and we must get home. It has been a long day. We will get some sleep and be ready for Agent Davis at the university. After that, where should we meet you and the rest of the team?"

I said, "I will call you," and I pointed to my head. Pete and his family were on the way home, so I decided that his family should meet us at the Tucson bank, and Pete agreed.

Jill said, "I feel different. My mind is opening. I can remember a lot of my childhood, my father, and when we lost my mother. Did I just hear Pete say, 'Okay'?"

"Here, Jill, have some food," said June. "Then you can shower and go to bed in our spare room. I will call you in the morning for breakfast and our trip to Tucson."

Stan asked, "Where are Bob, the kittens, and I going to sleep? We used to sleep on the floor under the bed in the spare bedroom."

"I like dogs and cats, so you can sleep under my bed tonight," Jill said.

"Jill, you need to leave the door open, since Bob is our night watch cat," I said. "She will defend the team and protect the children. Do you remember the story last year about the cat who ran a child molester up a cactus? That cat was Bob."

"I do remember," replied Jill. "I think I am going to like this new job more than any other job I've ever had."

The next morning, June came into the kitchen and said, "Bobby and Robby are sleeping with Jill, so I woke them all. I guess Stan is out with Bob."

I said, "That is all right. Let us all sit down around the table." When Jill came into the room, I said to the team, "Let us all think with our open minds and call Stan and Bob to breakfast."

The thought that came back to our minds said, *"Do not start without us."*

Jill said, "I am going to like this job."

After breakfast, we loaded up everything that we needed to open a bank account and get Jill in place to help the team. Then I said, "Jill, you are an independent contractor in Tucson's financial district. You will circulate through the district and put your resume out as though you are looking for clients. Your potential clients will want to do a background check on you, but you should not worry. Your clear background check and experience will land you any job. You will move into a nice apartment, get a phone, and be ready for more work. You will transfer your money from

Ajo to the bank of your choice. You will be notified when you are needed. An FBI agent named Davis will do your background check, so you will be in good hands."

Then June said, "Let's eat, so that we will be ready to cross the reservation."

In the meantime, Pete, Angel, and Mike were on their way to Tucson. Pete had told John and Manuel to stay home and wait for a call from him when everything was complete at the university. Pete, Angel, and Mike arrived at the university in record time for their meeting with the regents and Special Agent Davis. At 1:30, Agent Davis and his partner, Agent Samson, approached the Garcias and greeted them.

Agent Davis said, "I assume that Russ told you to let me do the talking."

"Yes, he did, and we will let you handle everything," said Pete. "Russ also told us that we can trust you and Agent Samson to help Mike get back in school."

"Do you have your team ID cards?" asked Agent Davis.

Pete said, "June was getting them ready for us last night in Ajo. I am sure we'll get them when we meet them at the Tucson bank later."

"That is good," replied Agent Davis, "as I do not want anyone to think that you are government employees. I am sure you will have to do that sometime in the future, but not now."

At two o'clock according to the clock on the wall, both agents went to the office door.

The receptionist said, "You cannot go in there. They are having a meeting."

However, the agents just waved their FBI IDs, opened the door, and motioned to the Garcias to follow them in.

Inside the office, the man at the head of the table stood up and asked, "What is the meaning of this?"

Davis answered, "We are here with the Garcia family for their two o'clock appointment with all of you who are sitting around this table. Why did you try to avoid them, and why are these people whom you like in your university? I think that since you are all here, you should vote to reinstate Mike Garcia, so that his family does not have to approach this problem another way. I think that you are unhappy that Mike's father, Pete

Garcia, helped uncover a problem with your treatment of sacred ground and that your teams were then escorted off the reservation. We are also here to make sure that you have returned everything to the tribal council. You have done that, I hope. Mr. Garcia will be checking on everything you have done about this matter. Okay, Pete, ask them about Mike's reinstatement."

Pete said, "Is my son welcome at this university? Is he the good student that he has always been? I think he wants to change the direction of his studies, so you should cooperate with him."

While the Garcias and Agent Davis were waiting for their appointment at the university, we were on the road to Tucson. I was watching Jill play with Bob's kittens; she was so full of love for those two young bobcats.

Bob said, "I think that I am going to lose one of my boys soon."

"What do you mean, Bob?" I asked.

"Just look at Jill with my Bobby and Robby," she said. "I know that Jill will be needing some protection in the city, so one of the team members should watch over her."

I asked, "Which one do you think should do it?"

"We will let them make that decision for themselves," replied Bob. "After all, they are members of the team now."

I turned to June and asked, "Do you have all the ID cards for the team?"

"Yes, I do," she replied.

"You should give Jill's card to her now," I said. "Jill, are you ready for this day? Now that you have your ID card, what do you think about it? Are you pleased to see that you are an agent of the United States government? Use this card as your identification when you rent an apartment or do anything pertaining to your shelter and protection. There is one more thing—you might need a watch cat at night. Talk to Robby and Bobby, and the three of you decide which of them will be your protector. On the back of your government ID, you will see that wildlife is one of your responsibilities. If you rent, you'll need the landlord's approval to have the cat there."

I drove into the Tucson bank's parking lot, and we left the cats in the car with the windows rolled down so that they could have fresh air and the car would not overheat. June put the Federal Wildlife parking tag in the window, and the cats stayed in their cage on the back seat, which Bob could open if necessary. The car would be safe.

We went into the bank and walked up to the desk, and I asked to see the bank manager. The clerk picked up her phone, pressed a button, and told the manager that three customers wanted to talk with him. He came right out and asked, "What can I do for you?"

I opened my wallet and showed him my government ID, as did June and Jill. Then I said, "We wish to open accounts here. Jill Anderson is our account manager, and she will help you set up the accounts." The manager took Jill over to a desk next to the receptionist, and she started with our accounts. Meanwhile I asked the receptionist if she could help Jill find an apartment in Tucson.

"I would love to help with anything that you need," she replied. "I will call my landlord. I know he has a two-bedroom available, so maybe she can move in today." She picked up her phone, dialed, and then said to someone, "Do you still have the two-bedroom? I have your renter here at the bank. She is a federal employee and would like to move in today. I will give her the address when she is finished here." Then she reached into her desk drawer, pulled out a business card for the apartment building, and handed it to me. She said, "The rest of your team will need to come in later today to complete their paperwork, but all the cashier checks have been accepted."

As we turned to leave, the three Garcias walked into the bank, and June and Jill handed them their ID cards. Jill walked them over and introduced them to the bank manager. Then she told him that the other Garcias were working, but that she would have them at the bank in the morning.

The next step was to rent Jill's apartment and decide which cat would be her protector. As we arrived at the Del Rancho apartment complex, the landlord was outside waving at us and directing us to a parking space. He said, "Jill, I will be your landlord."

Jill said, "Let us see the apartment, and then you might become my landlord if the apartment is satisfactory."

He said, "My name is Sam Williams, and the apartment is on the second floor of this office building, just over mine. Follow me, please."

We all followed him into the apartment, and then Jill said, "Russ and

June, this place will do. It is nice and close to the banking district. Mr. Williams, where do we sign the lease?"

He said, "We can do our business right here, and then you can move in immediately. You will be living here alone, but do you have any pets? The rent is $550 a month, with one month in advance plus $300 cleaning, so that will be $1,400 to move in today."

Jill asked, "Where am I going to get that much money today?"

"Well, will my check on the Tucson bank be okay?" asked June.

Sam replied, "Oh yes, I have many bank employees living here. In fact, you were recommended by my longest renter."

As we went to get Jill's bags and the one box, I turned to Robby and Bobby and asked, "Which of you is going to stay with Jill? Please get into the cage, so that we can get you moved into your new home." The two boys looked at each other, and then Bobby jumped into the cage.

As we went up the stairs, the landlord said, "I thought you said no pets."

Jill replied, "This is a bobcat who has problems, as you can read on the lease. As my ID says, I am supposed to help return these young cats to the wild. Do I move in with this federally protected bobcat, or do I go somewhere else?"

He quickly said, "Oh, please stay here."

When we got everything into Jill's apartment, I said, "There is a store just across the street on the corner. You can feed Bobby anything that you eat, if it has some blood in the meat. He loves canned fish and several other things, though he will tell you that you are wrong about his diet. And please, no salty potato chips. Don't forget the phone."

Jill replied, "Have I ever forgotten anything that you have told me?"

"No," I said, "you haven't, and let us keep it that way."

Back at the university, Mike went to his adviser's office and asked to change his major. His adviser asked, "Mike, why are you here? You were terminated by the board last week, so you have no business being here now."

Mike said, "I was reinstated yesterday. You should get in touch with the board. I am here to change my major to archaeology, and you should note that I have a government ID. As an agent of the archaeology department, I am to continue with my education at this university, and you need to make this happen today. Call the board now, and they will tell you what to do in my case. My top priorities are to prepare for artifacts, wildlife, plants, insects, and other unusual problems such as ghosts that terrify professors at their digs—like the professor who was on the reservation a while back and the two young ladies at the national park."

Mr. Smith, the adviser, made his call and said, "I have Mike Garcia in my office. What should I do with him?"

Mike could hear the answer even without a phone. "Do what he wants, and do not intimidate him in any way. That young man has the authority of the federal government behind him, so do whatever he wants."

Mr. Smith said, "I will set up the new plan of study for a bachelor's degree in archaeology. Also, I will interface for you with all the professors in that department, plus others who will be needed in the other fields that you noted. I did write them down, so you can go now and come back here on Friday. By the way, who is paying for this change?"

Mike said, "Me, my father, and my sponsor. I think you knew the answer before you asked."

Chapter 4

Moving to the other side of the mountain

The team had a meeting with everyone but Mike, who was still at the university. Pete asked, "What do you think he is doing?"

Russ answered, "He is being alpha to the professors in the archaeology department and loving every moment of it."

Then June said, "This meeting will come to order. We are here to get back to work on the cave of the little people. We need their help while we are looking for the lost treasures of the Native Americans—north, central, and south."

I said, "We need to get set up again on the west side of the Ajo Mountain Range. If that is not possible, then over the mountain to the reservation side. I am sure the tribal council will be more than happy if we are on their side of the mountain range. They know that if we find anything related to their myths and legends, we will make sure they get the prize. We will be able to inspect the ten digs on the tribal lands."

Pete said, "Mike and his brothers can do a lot of the inspections during his time off. Jill, what will you be doing?"

Jill answered, "Setting up my place of work in Tucson. The bank has a vacant office on the eighth floor where I can do the banking business that Russ said I should do. As you can see, Bobby is one happy cat. It is difficult to keep people from visiting us announced. The landlord has his ear to the door when I am in the apartment. He seems to be afraid of Bobby, which is good."

June said, "We have many things to do this week, so I suggest that we give it a good start in the morning."

In the morning, I set out for the National Park Headquarters to see if we could have a space to continue our survey. Pete and I arrived at the same time, and we went into the office and made our request. The chief ranger said, "I'm sorry, but the campgrounds are full. As you can see, the weather is wonderful, and the campers are plenty."

We thanked him and then drove both vehicles to the reservation to see our friend the chief council member. We asked him for a place on the east side of the Ajo Mountain Range so that we could survey the area where lost mines were indicated on our maps. Some mines were Spanish, others Mexican, and the biggest one, Montezuma's Treasure, was well known in the West.

The chief smiled and said, "Oh yes, over there by Manager's Dam. I understand that you have old friends there. I am sure they will help you and your team get set up."

"That will be great," I said. "How is the electricity in that neighborhood? We now have four air-conditioned tents and a generator, so we will not have to use any of the tribe's power. However, we might need a runner occasionally to bring us gasoline for the generator and a tank for water— just enough for the team on the site. Also, maybe a police officer to check on us now and then, although we do have some protection even without guns. You met Stan, my dog, and several of his friends that day in Spider Valley."

The chief said, "Yes, good friends like that can scare the shit out of people. I do believe you are a shaman, like you told me, to make a grown man climb a cactus."

"We will be here with tents for sleeping and a lab," I said, "with some food supplies if the villagers let us cook. I do not need to gain any weight while we are working out here. For your information, we have an office at the Tucson bank where one of our team members is stationed. She manages our bank accounts and takes care of wildlife and other things. Mike is at the university doing a good job for his tribe. He is studying archaeology, all about the history of Native Americans."

Later, Pete asked, "Where are we going to get the stuff that you told the chief about?"

"GSA," I replied. "Where else do you think we could get what we need for the job we were hired to do?"

We went to the Federal Building and asked to have our list of equipment delivered to Manager's Dam on the reservation. The delivery was scheduled for the following Monday, so we had a few days to clean up our climbing gear, tools, shovels, and pickaxes.

On Monday morning, we all met at Pete's house. Then, along with our favorite tribal chief, we drove to Manager's Dam, hoping to get started on our search for another entrance to the cave of the little people.

As we arrived in Manager's Dam, a man about John's age walked up to the chief and said, "I am John Jones. I have been picked to help these people while they are here. I will be their runner."

The chief said, "John, this is your godmother's son, Russ Philips."

John looked at me and said, "My mother will be happy that you will be with us. She is living here in the village. You must come with me to meet her, as she is sick."

Everyone waited while I walked with John to visit his mother. When she and I saw each other, she told John to call his brother, Russ, to join us. Then she said to me, "Russ, you haven't changed at all."

I held her hand and said, "Your niece Angel and her husband, Pete, are here with me and my wife, June. We will be on this site for a while, so we can have a good fiesta with you and your family and friends."

She said, "You were always a good boy, and I loved your mother for what she did for my people. Don't wait too long for that fiesta, as I don't have much time left."

Just then, John and his brother, Russ, entered the room. John said to me, "Two trucks are on their way here, about a mile away." Then he said to his brother and said, "Russ, meet Russ."

Russ turned to his mother and asked, "Is he the one?"

"Yes, he is," she replied.

Everyone at Manager's Dam seemed to know who I was. The adult men came and said, "We will help you, for we all loved your mother." I had a tear in my eye as I listened to them praise my mother.

When the trucks arrived, one of the drivers asked, "Where do you want us to unload your equipment?"

I turned to my new friend, John Jones, and asked, "Where is the best place to place our four tents and power generator so that the noise won't disturb your people?"

John said, "See that flat place to the west? Over there you will have enough room for your camp and not be too far from your new family. It looks like we are all family, now that my brothers have met the son of our godmother."

The truck driver said, "It looks like we can drive the load over there." The two trucks were driven to the site and unloaded. The two drivers did all the heavy work, placing the generator on a level place so that its platform was secure. Then they set up the platforms for the tents and even assembled the tents for us, so the day was complete,

Some of the village members came up to us before the trucks left and said, "Mrs. Jones wants all of you to stay and have a meal with us. We're having a celebration of the family get-together tonight."

The lead truck driver asked, "Are we invited too?"

"Yes, I am sure that you are," I said. "You worked hard today, and you need to relax, but you drivers should not touch the wine. You can have a good time at a fiesta without wine."

We decided to set up our sleeping quarters so that we could get some sleep, as we had had too much wine with our meal. No one should drive after even one swallow of cactus wine. John Garcia had been smart to pack our beds in his van. I loved that team because their minds were always working. We got the generator running so that we had lights and could see what we are doing, and then we just went to bed.

In the morning, John Jones called through the tent door, "Mom says breakfast is ready, so come and eat."

We got dressed as fast as we could, as we did not want to displease Mom. After rushing over to her house, we were welcomed with bacon, eggs with chili peppers, and coffee.

As we sat around the table, June said, "Angel and I need to go to Ajo and buy some food supplies. We do not want to impose on Mom or any other family members here in Manager's Dam every day. You know, you men eat at strange hours when you are working, and we never know what or where you eat."

Pete said, "Today we look for a cave. John Jones, do you know of any caves on this side of the Ajo Mountain Range?"

John answered, "If I can look at your map, I should be able to show you some sites, even though I have not been there for years."

Mom said, "John, you hunted in that range for deer. You said that when you saw the sacred cave of our people, you saw a wildcat go into the cave. Then you changed your mind and did not want to go in."

Russ took the map out of his map case and said, "Here, John, mark the map, and that will be our start on this side."

As Pete and I started out, we decided to take his pickup truck to save time, since the hike would take half our day. We soon arrived at the canyon that John marked for us on the map. We had Bob with us for our investigation of this small box canyon, so I said, "Bob, use your experience and help us find this cave."

In our minds, we heard Bob say, *"Open your minds and remember that you can see what is just ahead of us."*

Pete said, "Holy cow, that is the cave. Let us go in and make sure we are back in the underworld of the Chichimecs. Then we can continue our search for the Aztec treasure."

As we walked into the cave, we turned on our lights so that we could see in the dark and announce to the Chichimecs that we were back to help them in their search. We intentionally made some noise, and I called out, "We are back on the east side of the mountain, and we would like another visit with your people."

Arriving at a room containing many native remains laid out in a logical method and wrapped in woven blankets, we realized that we were in the sacred cave that Mom had told us was in this mountain. There were no treasures with the remains—just a few jars and rusty cans of food for the dead as they crossed into the next world. It did not look like anyone had visited the cave in many years.

As we left that grave cave, we met our old friend, the chief of the Chichimecs, who asked, "Why do you enter the cave of the dead?"

I said, "We were not able to use the other entrance. Too many people of the upperworld are on the west side, so we came this way to keep you safe."

The chief said, "Follow me," and led us through the cave to some paintings on the wall that were like those in the cave on the west side.

I asked, "Chief, can we look over these paintings and take some photos to study when we return to the upperworld?"

"Yes," he said, "and as you did in the other cave, call me when you finish with this search. Then I will send a warrior to escort you to the rest of us."

Pete said, "I am glad I used one roll of film on the burial ground when we passed through that cave. I have about six rolls of film in my bag, so I will start at the beginning. How many rolls of film do you have, Russ?"

"Only five," I said.

As we took pictures of the walls, Pete asked, "How long have we been in here today?"

I said, "According to my watch, we have been looking around and taking pictures about twelve hours since arriving at the cave. Are you hungry?"

"After twelve hours, I should be very hungry," Pete said, "but I am not. Are you sure that your watch is right?"

"I don't know," I replied. "Do you remember the last time we were in the cave of the Chichimecs? We thought we were in the cave for one day, but we were there for a week. Let us finish up here and call for our escort to the chief."

We packed up our gear and made our call. After what seemed like five minutes, a warrior came to get us. We followed him for what seemed like four hours, until finally we were in the large room that we had seen on our previous visit.

The chief said, "We welcome our friends from the upperworld, and we again thank you for your efforts to locate the Aztec treasure. We have spent many years searching for it. What do you have to report to us?"

I answered, "Mike, one of Pete's sons, is looking through records on the history of the Aztecs at the university. We now have a history of your picture walls, and we will need some time to translate your language into English. We should be able to tell you more after we study the photos we took today."

Then we were escorted to the entrance on the east side of the mountain.

When we emerged from the cave, John Jones was waiting for us. Bob was with him, rubbing her head on his hand.

I asked, "John, why are you here?"

"You two have been in that cave for two weeks," said John. "This bobcat was here too, and it looks like she has been waiting for you. She is too friendly for a wildcat, but she hunts like I have never seen before. She brought me a rabbit and then ran off to get one for herself. She seemed to know that I was hungry."

I looked at Bob and asked, "Why did you leave the cave?"

Not wanting to talk, Bob thought, *"I did not like the dead, and you were too busy to pay attention to me. So, I came out here to wait for you and Pete. This man whom you call John has been waiting here with me, so I made friends with him because he is your friend. He waited, so I hunted rabbits for us to eat. He skinned his rabbit and then built a fire to cook it, but as you know, I don't like cooked meat."*

I said to John, "Yes, this bobcat is my incredibly good friend. I am glad that she brought you the rabbit and birds to eat, but why didn't you eat the lizard?"

John asked, "How did you know about the lizard? When you and the cat were bumping heads, what did she tell you?"

"Look at the bird feathers, rabbit skins, and all those lizard tails," I replied. "You need to keep your campsite clean, John. Otherwise, everybody will know what you have eaten. Okay, now we need to get back to base camp to develop these films and get them ready for the code busters."

We all got into the pickup and headed back to our base camp. Riding in the back of the truck, John shook his head and said, "I don't believe it. Russ knew what that bobcat and I ate just by looking at our campsite."

Pete and I tried not to make too much noise laughing at John. If he had only known.

Bob said, *"Leave that young man alone. He has a good heart."*

When we arrived at the tents, John got off the truck and walked over to his mom's house.

June came out and said, "Mom said John was probably with you in that cave."

I looked at June and said, "Pete and I were in the cave the whole time, and Bob was with us for a little while at first. We took photos of the sacred

78

grave cave for our records. According to my watch, we were in the cave forty-eight hours. Right, Pete?"

June and Angel glanced at each other, and then June said, "You were gone two weeks, and you had Mom so worried. We were also worried that you might be in danger, so we sent John to find you, and then Mom got all upset."

"Well, John just went into Mom's house," I replied. "She will always be upset when any of her children do anything unknown to her, because that is just what mothers do. Bob has a new friend, and she made John happy by catching wildlife for them to eat. You can ask John what was on the menu. I am not sure he will tell you what her hunting was like."

"On another note," I continued, "we took photos of the remains in the grave cave, and of the writing on the wall of the cave on the east side of the Ajo Mountain Range. The writing on that sacred cave wall is in neither the Chichimec language nor any other native language that I have ever seen. We need to get the photos and negatives to our team in Washington, DC, right away for a translation. I think we need to go to Tucson and get them on a plane to DC immediately. I don't know what this writing is, but it is different."

When Pete called out for Angel and June to go to the lab right away, the ladies asked, "What is up? Are you going tonight?"

I said, "No, not tonight, but as soon as we get the photos developed. We may have to explain what we found over the last two weeks. I showed them the first picture of the sacred cave. Of the Papago People? Maybe, but maybe not. Look at the writing on the wall."

"Yes, it is different from the first batch," June agreed. "What language do you think it is?"

I said, "I don't know. All I can do is guess, and my guess is that it is from the old world or another world. We will go to Tucson if we get all these photos developed."

We all worked through the day and night to develop our many wall photos. When Mom sent Russ over to invite us to dinner at her house, we decided to take a break and go, especially since Mom's food was always excellent. When we finished dinner, we thanked our hostess.

"Thank you for having your bobcat take care of John this past week," she replied.

I told her that she had a very loyal family, and then we went back to the lab to complete our work.

When we got to the lab, John Jones was waiting for us. "Can I see the pictures of the sacred cave?" he asked.

I said, "Sure, John, come on into the lab." We went inside, and I handed him a photo of the writing on the wall.

"The last time I saw this in the cave," said John, "it sent chills down my spine. I ran away because I had told Mom that I had seen a bobcat but did not go inside the cave. I don't like it when I don't tell her the truth."

I asked, "What did you see?"

"I saw a little man dressed strangely. He looked at me and just kept moving away, like I scared him too." Then John asked, "Did you see any little men in the cave taking care of the dead under the covers of all those dead people?"

"No," I replied, "and you should not say anything about that. John, have you seen any writing like this anywhere around here?"

"Sure, there are rocks all over with markings like this."

"Will you take us to where these painted rocks are in the morning?" I asked.

"Yes sir, but I have to get Mom's permission to take you there," John said. "She gets upset when any of us boys go into the desert alone without telling her where we are going."

I said, "That is a good thing to do, John. We should be through with this preliminary work by morning, and then we will take a trip into the desert with our guide. Go tell Mom, and then go on to bed. I am not sure when we will be finished here. We will need some rest before we go to Tucson tomorrow to use the secure phone line in Jill's apartment to make our call about this discovery."

After about four hours of sleep, we were awakened by the smell of eggs and bacon being cooked. We took some time to see how the negatives and pictures were drying, and then we all had a great breakfast of eggs, bacon, and coffee. John Jones came up to us while we were eating and asked, "What time will we be going into the desert to see the painted rocks? Some are large, and others are the size of a book."

I said to the team, "John is taking us to a place in the desert where there are painted stones that may have similar markings to those in the cave." Then we finished packing for our trip. I told Stan that we were taking Bob with us to Jill and Bobby's apartment, and she agreed to stay with the ladies.

We got into our four-wheel-drive pickup truck and set out into the desert southwest of Manager's Dam. About six miles from camp, John said, "Not much farther. Just on the other side of the dry creek bed." We slowed down to cross the sandy bottom of the creek and then arrived at the first large boulder, which was about seven feet in diameter.

John jumped out of the truck cab and said, "Look, I told you! See the chipped marks on this rock? They are like the marks in the cave, so this must be sacred ground too. Come with me, and I will show you smaller rocks, the size of a book, with marks on all sides."

Pete asked, "John, would you mind if we took one of these rocks to our lab and maybe then to Tucson, and in the meantime take some photos of the rocks here?"

"Take what you need," John replied. "I know you will help our people keep our sacred places free from those university thieves."

I finished photographing the rocks and marking their locations, so that if we returned to that site, we would have a record starting on that date. Then I said, "Thank you, John. You are a good son of your tribe. You always have them in mind, and you want them to learn about their history and all the artifacts on this land."

Then I turned to Pete and said, "We need to get John back to the village, tell the ladies that we are on our way, and pick-up Bob to take with us to visit Bobby." John asked who Bobby was, and Pete said, "Just another cat."

We dropped John in Manager's Dam and then drove up to our campsite to tell our wives goodbye and collect Bob. Then we headed out to the highway to Tucson to make our report.

When we arrived at Jill's, she met us at the door of her apartment and said, "Please, come in. You too, Bob. Bobby is in the bedroom. Why are you all here today? I have not heard a word, and I have been wondering if I still have a job, though paychecks are regularly deposited in my bank account. It is good to see you."

I said, "Jill, I need to use the secure phone."

"I thought the kitchen table would be the best place for it," she replied. "Follow me."

We all went into the kitchen and sat down, and I asked, "Jill do you have any coffee? We would like a cup if you did."

"Only instant coffee. Will that be okay?" she replied.

Pete said, "Make mine strong, Jill. Russ, how about you?"

"Yes, strong will be okay," I said. "Black, no sugar, and no cream."

As Jill began heating the water and put the coffee in the cups, Bob and Bobby came in the kitchen and sat at the table with us. Trying not to upset Jill, Bob said through her mind, *"Bobby reports that there has been a lot of activity in this apartment complex that worries Jill. Neighbors have been trying to get her to remove her clothes and jump into the pool with them. They call her a prude, whatever that is—even the lady who told her about this apartment."*

Jill said, "Bobby, are you telling them my problems? You should know by now that I can hear what you are saying in your mind. And yes, Russ, it is getting harder for me to control my temper. Sometimes I just want to yell at them to leave me alone."

Bobby thought, *"She won't let me tear them apart. But if they ever get into this apartment, I will not ask for permission. I will just protect my lady."*

I told them I would take care of the problem if Jill wanted me to.

Jill asked, "But Russ, what can you do?"

So, I picked up the phone and made my call to DC. A voice answered, "Hello, Russ. What can I do to help you and your team?"

First, I reported on our findings at the Ajo Mountain Range—the photos, the writings on the walls of the sacred cave, and the rocks scattered around the desert. I explained that we needed to get our reports and one rock to our examiners of ancient writing.

"An air force officer will be there today to pick up those things and deliver them to us," replied the voice. "Now, is there anything else?"

I said, "Yes, one more thing. Agent Jill Anderson, my team's contact here in Tucson, is being harassed at her apartment complex. She is trying to keep a low profile because of our business here in southern Arizona. What can we do to keep her safe? She refuses to participate in their dirty games, and we do not want to have to move out of here."

He answered, "I will take care of that problem right now. You must not do anything, as we need to keep you out of the news. Have a good week, Russ. It would be great if you could report weekly. Sometimes on this project you seem to lose time between calls."

I said, "Yes, I know. As I reported previously, we are working in several different time zones. Goodbye for now." Then I hung up the phone, turned to Jill, and said, "I do not yet know how, but DC will take care of your problem here at the apartment complex. We are to do nothing about this ourselves, but just to keep doing our job and let DC do theirs."

As we sat around waiting for the air force, we got hungry. Jill said, "Tomorrow is my shopping day. I don't have enough food here to feed everyone today."

Pete said, "I will get us some takeout from that restaurant across the street," and I reminded him to get some raw meat for the cats."

As Pete left the apartment, I watched him walk across the parking lot to the street corner. Some men at the pool got up and watched old man Pete cross the street, and then looked up toward Jill's apartment—and slapped their butts. It was obvious that they were upset about seeing Pete come out of the apartment.

Pete got back to the apartment just as the air force officer arrived with two armed airmen. We heard Pete say, "Thank you for coming to help us."

The officer knocked on the door, rather than ringing the doorbell, and came inside, leaving the two airmen waiting outside. "I am Captain Lewis," he said. "You have something for me to take to DC? I have armed protection with me to help keep everything safe." Handing a case to Jill, he asked, "Will it all fit in this case?"

Jill turned to me and said, "What do you think, Boss?"

"Let me see," I replied, picking up my case. "I am transferring the items into your case, officer. Then you will sign this paper saying that we have made the transfer, and we will both seal the locking device. I will keep the signed release, and you have the artifacts."

The officer called out, "Sergeant, take this case. You two men return to the van with the case, and I will be with you in a minute." As we watched the airmen carry the case away, the officer turned to Jill and said, "It will always be a pleasure to serve you. Goodbye."

As he walked out the door, Jill looked at Pete and asked, "What was that?"

Pete said, "Dear lady, that was a gentleman."

Just as we sat down to eat our meal, the doorbell rang. When I opened the door, there stood Agents Davis and Samson.

Davis said, "What can we do to help you, Russ?"

I asked, "What were you told?"

"Well, our boss in Washington said that you would tell us what to do," he replied.

I said, "Okay, you see those people around the pool? They have been harassing this young agent, Jill Anderson. I would like the two of you to make them stop."

Davis replied, "We have no authority to do that without a complaint from the victim."

I said, "Do you mean to tell me that you can't go out there and question them? Take down their names and explain that the woman in this apartment is a federal agent. They need to leave her alone, and if they continue to harass her, they will be subject to the law."

Davis said, "Okay, I will give it a try. I will warn them not to interfere in any way with a federal agent who is performing her duty. It is legal for me, with my badge, to caution anyone who is harassing an agent or civilian. We will take their names down and get the local police to check on their license plates. That should keep them away from Jill."

"Just do not say or do anything to bring the press into this problem," I added.

Now that we could finally get back to our meal, Jill volunteered to warm it up for us.

After we ate, I said, "Look at Bob and Bobby. They did like their red meat, and now they are cleaning each other." Turning to Jill, I said, "You must call Agent Davis if the harassment resumes. Now, if you look out your window at the pool, you will see two bad FBI agents doing their job."

Pete and I needed to get back to the reservation, but we decided to spend the night at the motel down the street from Jill's apartment. In the morning, we would check on Jill, pick up Bob, and head back to the base camp and our wives. After we checked in, I called Jill, told her where we were, and gave her the phone number for the motel. I felt okay for the night, especially knowing that two bobcats were in that apartment with her, but I knew that I needed to make other long-term arrangements for her and Bobby.

Following our 6:00 a.m. wake-up call, we got cleaned up and went to the motel office to turn in the key. The motel manager opened the door and said, "A Miss Jill called, but I guess you did not know that, since you are here. She was upset and crying, and she needs help."

Before he could finish the message, Pete and I were running to the truck. At Jill's apartment complex, a police vehicle was blocking the parking lot. The officer standing there said, "Show me some ID, and tell me what you two are here for."

I told the officer, "Jill is one of our team members, and she just called me for help. Can we see her?"

"You will need clearance from the sergeant in charge of this case," he replied.

"Well, then get him here," I insisted, "and call the person listed on this card. He needs to be here as well."

The officer looked at the card and said, "This is FBI Agent Davis. We know him, and I would like to get him away from breakfast. I will be mad, but he will be glad that you requested his presence."

The sergeant came out to talk to us and asked, "What kind of federal agents are you two men and Miss Anderson?"

I answered, "That information is on our ID cards. We are special agents for the search and recovery of artifacts, animal wildlife, and rare plant life. Have you called FBI Agent Davis? He is one of our team members."

Then the sergeant said, "So that is why she has two bobcats in her apartment and their cage doors are open."

"Sergeant, just what is the problem here?" I asked. "Has Jill been hurt? I need to see her. Did the bobcats get out of control?"

The sergeant replied, "Yes, you might say that. We have Animal Control coming to pick them up."

I said, "No, they can't do that. Those two bobcats are protected by the federal government, and Agent Davis will take over this crime scene. Your presence will be limited to what you need to know."

When we finally got into the apartment, I asked Jill, "What happened?"

She said, "Those two assholes you saw at the pool yesterday broke into the apartment, and Bob responded the way she was trained. She jumped from her cage and used her claws on one man. The other man pulled a gun, and Bobby responded just like his mother had, ripping into the hand that held the gun. Then the two big bad men started crying. They were stretched out on the floor, and the cats were sitting on their backs, just waiting for you and Pete to show up. The landlord called the police, and that sergeant has been an asshole, but I think he must be a good cop."

Just as she finished, Agent Davis walked into the room that was not bloody and said, "Russ, I knew it was you. Can you fill me in?"

Jill repeated what she had told me and gave a formal statement about what had happened during the break-in.

Then Davis said to me, "Russ, you have your team well trained. I wish you could spend some time helping with my team."

"Be careful what you ask for," I replied.

Then the police sergeant came in and said, "Animal Control is here to pick up the cats."

Agent Davis asked, "Why are you going to remove these bobcats? They were doing their job by keeping this woman safe. Do you remember that man in Ajo who got run up a cactus when he tried to molest a little girl? Well, I want you to meet the bobcat who does what she has been trained to do. She is under study by Mr. Philips and his team, and Miss Anderson, a team member, oversees these cats. There is also a third cat, and Mrs. Philips is investigating unknown factors about wild animals. By the way, sergeant, you, and your team will face federal charges if you do not treat this as top-secret information. Now I will take charge of the two men who assaulted three federal agents. I warned them yesterday, but they did not listen to me."

The sergeant told one of his officers to turn the two men over to the FBI. "Also, give FBI Agent Davis and his people all the evidence that we have collected, as this case is no longer any of our concern. I will take care of all reports, and you men just forget what happened here."

I went back into the kitchen and said, "Jill, I think that you need a short rest at our base camp back at Manager's Dam, complete with some time with our wives and Mom's cooking. That will be a good break for Mom and Bobby. Pete and I will help you pack up. I know that you will need help to get past this attack on you and the cats. Mom, June, and Angel will be a good support group, and Mom's young men will be there to help you with anything you need. They are well behaved, as they never want to upset Mom. The team, of course, will stand with you always. You,

Stan, and Robby will need to help Bobby understand that he did his job and helped his mother take down those two intruders. I do not think that you will need to be present at the trial of the two men who broke into your apartment. The taped statement that you gave Agent Davis should persuade them to confess to the crime, and after Davis completes his thorough investigation, they should ask for a plea deal."

Pete came in and said, "The cats are in the truck in their cage. Where are Jill's bags and other stuff? We need to get going, as we will be driving into the sun. It has taken a long time with the police and FBI."

I closed Jill's cases, and she picked up the records in her file. As we were leaving the apartment, we were stopped by the landlord, who complained about the damage to the apartment. I told him that he would need to contact the FBI or any government official about his claim, and I warned him that they would ask, "Do you have the PO for your safety system before the damage? Who installed the devices, and where were they installed? They need to be up to US security standards." Then we walked away, leaving the landlord standing there looking puzzled.

Just before turning onto Ajo Way, we stopped at a drive-in restaurant to get food for the road. While we were there, we brought Bob and Bobby into the cab with us and asked what they wanted to eat. They both said red meat, which made Jill smile. "Their answer never changes," she said, "and isn't it great to hear Bobby talking now?"

Pete and I ate our hamburgers on the road, and Jill had fried potatoes. About halfway to base camp, the sun started to get in our eyes, so we were glad to have sunglasses. By the time we finally came to the road south to Manager's Dam, the mountain helped us with a little shade for the last few miles.

When we arrived at base camp, June and Angel were sitting around our camp table playing with Robby and stroking Stan. June exclaimed, "You are back and safe, and you brought Jill! What happened? You were only supposed to be in Tucson one day."

I said, "Jill was attacked in her apartment. Agent Davis has the two men in federal jail, but Jill will need all the support we can give her."

Angel asked, "What did the bastards do to her?"

Pete answered, "One man pulled a gun, so Bobby took his hand off, while Bob took the other man down with more claw marks than that man who ran up the cactus. Davis said that both cats did the job they were trained to do, and he told the police and Animal Control to take a hike and keep their mouths shut. That man has a wonderful way of saying things. He had already warned the two men that Jill was a federal agent and that it is a felony to follow her or keep track of her. But then they broke into her apartment with guns, intending to do harm, so our protectors had an opportunity to use their skills for good again."

When Pete asked if the boys were around, Angel said, "No, since you and Russ were using John Jones, they went home when you two went into the cave."

I said, "Then Jill can use their tent tonight. Also, Mom could be a help with the three of you ladies and a real benefit for Jill, sort of like a fiesta Mom's way. I am sure she will be a good friend, and we can send John Jones to get food for the fiesta and bring our boys back to camp. We can decide for Jill to use the lab after we get her a folding bed. By the way, what is for supper? This day took a lot out of us, and we are tired and need to relax. Tomorrow we'll need to plan for the next cave trip."

The next morning, we had a good breakfast cooked by Angel with help from June and Jill. After we finished our meal and cleaned up the table, I saw John Jones walking toward camp. When he arrived, I said, "John, you need to meet Jill Anderson, who will be staying with us for a few days. Would you take her to meet Mom? After all, I did request a festa to welcome her to the village and make her feel at home."

"Okay," said John, "I will be happy to take Jill to Mom's. The reason I am here is to tell you that Mom would like some help with the cooking."

All three ladies agreed, and Pete and I went with his two sons to the lab to plan our next trip into the cave. We agreed that Pete and Manuel would study the sacred cave, while John and I would visit the chief of the Chichimecs in the large cave in the center of the mountain. This exploration would begin after the fiesta for Jill, if we were able to start that soon—which depended on how much cactus wine the four of us consumed at the fiesta.

At the fiesta, I overheard John say to his father, "Thank you and Russ for planning to include us in this trip into the mountain." This made everyone smile.

Everyone had fun singing and dancing at the fiesta. I had forgotten how many people were coming, and when Mom noticed me looking puzzled, she said, "Russ, this is the whole village."

"I guess I just have not had enough wine yet," I said, still puzzled.

Mom said, "Try the wine on this table. It was made for your party by old man Gomez, and it is incredibly good. Take a bottle over to your team's table and pass it around."

I did, and then we all had more fun. Jill was the first to pass out, and Mom had me take her into one of the bedrooms and put her on the bed. The rest of us weaved back and forth as we walked back to our camp, and then I said, "Ladies and gentlemen, it looks like we have another day of rest."

The next morning, as we recovered from our party, I saw Jill walk up to our camp. Shaking her head, she asked, "What happened last night? Mom said that you put me to bed in her bed and she watched over me all night. Then I had a wonderful breakfast with no headache."

We were having coffee, and Angel asked Jill, "Would you like a cup of our campfire coffee?"

Jill replied, "No, I had enough coffee at Mom's this morning, and now I am so relaxed that I think I could do most anything."

We all knew that Mom had given us some of the special cactus wine the previous night, which meant that she wanted us to be safe on our trip into the cave. We had received a blessing from her and the great spirit, to come home in safety under the power of the gods. Before we started our journey by truck to the foothills of the Ajo Mountain, we wanted to wait for Jill to come down from the effects of the wine.

Chapter 5

Called to Washington D.C.

A truck with flashing red lights and a siren drove up, and the tribal police officer got out, walked up to the team, and said, "I have a message for you, Russ, from Washington, DC. It is marked as urgent, so I've brought it to you, and I am to wait for any return message."

I said to the officer, "Where is the horse I saw you on last time?"

"So, you recognize my new horse," he replied.

"Go see June," I said. "She can get you some coffee while you wait." Then I called for the rest of the team to join me in the lab, where I opened the large envelope and took out the papers and photos. Spreading them on the table, I asked Jill to read the message.

The first words out of her mouth were "Russ Philips, please stop all exploration on your current site. We need you in Washington ASAP. Your team is to watch over the site until you return."

Included in the envelope were some photos of a women whom I did not recognize. So, I opened the door of the lab and called out to June to pack my bag, because I would be going to Washington as I had been ordered. I told the team that they needed to follow the orders that they had just heard from Washington. Two of them should be posted at the cave openings on each side of the mountain, and someone needed to watch the rocks in the valley. They should use John Jones if necessary, and one driver was to keep all sites within sight until I returned.

Then I went to my tent and dressed for the trip. Walking over to the truck, I put my bag inside and said to the policeman, "Here is my return message: 'Get me to the air force base in Tucson as fast as you can. I have a plane to catch.'"

The officer said, "Yes sir, Mr. Philips." He turned on the siren and flashing red lights, and we were on our way in a cloud of dust. When I asked if we needed gas, he replied, "No, I have forty gallons in the second tank. We do not have many gas stations on the tribal lands, so we have big tanks."

When we arrived at the air force base, I showed the sergeant at the gate my ID card. He took it and made a call on his phone, and then returned to where we were parked and told the tribal policeman that he could return to the reservation.

The policeman turned to me and asked, "Mr. Philips, is it okay to leave you here with this sergeant?" I told him that it was fine and saluted him. Then he unloaded my bag and placed it next to the sergeant.

As I waited at the gate, a staff car drove up and a familiar-looking officer said, "Mr. Philips, your plane is ready, so we can go now. I will be your pilot, and you will recognize some of my crew. By the way, I was told that the fewer people who know about this, the better. You must have found something that they want."

Upon arrival at Andrews Air Force Base, we were taken by helicopter to the Pentagon and escorted into a large conference room. Most of the chairs were occupied, and I was directed to what looked like the head of the large round table. My name and rank were listed on a piece of paper at my seat. When the man to my right called the meeting to order, I recognized his voice and relaxed a bit.

"Russ Philips has made some very interesting finds on the reservation that he has been exploring for his government," he said. "He has put together a tiptop team to help him with his work, including his own wife, a banker, a retired miner, and the miner's wife and their four sons. Russ and his wife are both retired sailors. The miner, a Native American, is his best friend, and the miner's wife, also Native American, once worked with Russ's parents. The tribal council regards Russ's mother as a saint, so many people carry the names of Russ's family, including his brothers and sisters. Russ has an ability that we have never seen on earth, and he works with us. He and his team work almost alone, except for the tribal police force and two FBI agents whom Russ tricked into watching over them. We have a video clip of Russ with the tribal officer who delivered him to the air force base at Tucson today, and you can see the officer's reluctance to leave Russ with the sergeant. When the officer was told that he was free to return to the reservation, he handed Russ's travel bag to the sergeant, drove about fifty feet, and stopped to watch the sergeant salute Russ, before finally driving away and returning to his reservation.

"I did not mention everyone on his team, whom he believes to be of this earth, inside and out. The team also includes a dog and a cat, who are usually with him or another team in the field. You all have heard the story of the cat in Ajo, Arizona, that put a child molester up a cactus—that was Russ's cat. The natives think that Russ is a witch doctor or shaman placed on the reservation to help them end the university's plundering of sacred artifacts. Russ has convinced the university that if the plundering continues, he will raise a ghost that is tied into Native American myth and legend. Russ has caused one professor to commit herself to a hospital, along with two of her students, following their activities in two different places on the tribal lands. Now Russ wants to know why we have called him here."

A man at the other end of the table said, "We think that a group of college professors can do a better job than this retired navy chief petty officer."

I asked, "Is there a bug in this room?"

The general said, "No, but why do you ask? Who would want that information?"

"Is that a fly landing and taking off from your head?" I asked.

"So, you have good eyesight," he said. "What good does that do you on a dig?"

I said, "I can see my friends and helpers better than most university professors. Would you like a demonstration?"

Everyone in the room laughed and said, "Yes, do it now."

So, I said, "Fly, will you help me? Go to the general's microphone and give us a big buzz, please." I waited a minute and then asked, "What is your problem, fly? Okay, I get it. Too many generals. So, buzz the microphone in front of the person where you are flying."

They watched the fly land on a microphone and make a loud buzzing sound with his wings, but then everyone said, "So what? Flies do that all the time."

So, I said to the fly, "Go and bring back all the flies you can muster," and suddenly the room filled with flies. Then I said, "Swarm in the air above this round table," and they all moved to the center of the room. Then I said to the flies, "Investigate my mind and see the thought that I have there for you. My thought is Lady Liberty, so form that image above the table." The swarm started to shift, and suddenly it looked like our beloved Lady Liberty was hovering in the air.

Chapter 6

The Army takes over

Looking around the table, I asked, "Can your professors do that? All they need to do is learn how to communicate with the flies." Then I said to the flies, "Now you can return to whatever you were doing and leave these people alone," and the flies departed as fast as they had appeared.

"So, you have proved that you can talk to flies and maybe all lower forms of life, but just what are you able to do with that?" the general asked.

I said, "I can tell all those roaches that live in your home to leave, and then I can send in some mice, if you would like. Now why did you call me here?"

They said, "We would like you to add a certain person to your team."

"The woman who is sitting next to you in the photo," I replied. "She will have to pass my test of her mental abilities and do other things, both in the upperworld and the underworld. Can she go into dark places and not panic? Can she travel with me back to my base camp on the reservation today? She will be out of touch with all her friends, as all outgoing messages will have to go through me and be reported in the records. Who will pay her? Does she know that she will not be in charge, but that she will be an intern for the next six months? I have other interns right now, but we will all try our best to welcome her to the team.

"Now, if we are finished here, I would like to return to the desert, so have the young intern ready for her six months of training and examination. I do hope that she is made of the right stuff. If she is married, her husband can come with her and go through the same training, if someone else takes care of the expenses for their six-month honeymoon. By the way, can she travel today? She'll need to dress for the desert heat and cold, since we work all the time though not often overnight."

The general said, "She has volunteered to go with you. She has all the gear she will need in her bag, as she is a lieutenant in the army."

"We don't allow uniforms of any kind," I said. "We work in civilian clothing and have nice clothes for our time off. Full-length trousers, long-sleeved shirts, and strong boots made for hiking and climbing—you know, like army boots. That is the only acceptable uniform. She can have her military ID and dog tags, and I will issue her a team ID when we get to camp. She will also need sleeping quarters equivalent to ours. The air force does make a good tent setup for us. We will need to increase the volume of water for the team—bathing, laundry, and feeding the team and trainees. We will see if she is a volunteer, and we try to make jobs as easy as possible."

The army went shopping for the lieutenant, so that her clothing would be strong enough for the rocks and digging for old artifacts on the reservation. We took off from DC about 6:00 p.m. the next day, and the young lieutenant was full of questions.

"My name is Nancy Green, and I am from Texas," she said. "I am happy that you are giving me this opportunity to work with you on your digs. It will make Momma happy when I tell her where I am stationed, since she is half Indian and I am a quarter Indian. I do hope that I will be a good team member so that I can tell Momma what I am doing."

I said, "You phoned your home in Texas last night. What did you tell them?"

Nancy said, "I told them that I am going to a place in a desert for a while. I said that I would call them when I could, but not for at least six months."

"That was good thinking," I said.

Then she asked, "How did you know that I phoned my family in Texas last night?"

I replied, "A little fly told me."

Just then our pilot said over the intercom, "We are over Tucson and in our approach for landing. The air force is waiting on the tarmac with a truck, tent, and water tank. They will take you to your site, set everything up, and return with what is not needed."

After we landed and deplaned, the master sergeant said, "I see that your team is growing."

I replied, "Master Sergeant, I'd like you to meet Lieutenant Nancy Green of the US Army." He snapped to attention and saluted Nancy.

Later she asked, "Will he talk to anyone about me?"

"No, he is a true American," I said. Then I told her that I was glad the sergeant had saluted her, because it would be a long time between salutes. We got into the truck cab with the master sergeant and were on our way to Manager's Dam.

Nancy asked, "Where is this place called Manager's Dam?"

The sergeant answered, "Almost on the other side of the world as we know it. I like to make these trips, as it reminds me of how beautiful this land is."

Chapter 7

Return to Managers Dam

"Russ, you said that we would be in the desert," said Nancy.

I smiled and said, "You will learn to survive in it and even like it. I knew a sailor who wanted to live on a beach somewhere, and he picked this place."

The sergeant asked, "Mr. Philips, did you know that I worked at the radar station in Ajo? And when I retire, I am going to take my wife back to her hometown." He told me that his wife's name was Gloria Watson, "and she told me that she had a crush on you in school and at church, but that you always seemed to be thinking of other things. She said that you ran away to the navy when you were just seventeen and came home only for your family."

As we approached the base camp, it was still daylight. We pulled the truck around the tents, and I took Nancy to meet Mom.

Nancy asked, "Why do you call her Mom when she is not your mother?"

"Well, you will find that Mom is the godmother of all her children. She is a good woman who deserves the same respect that she gives to me and my mother."

"Oh, so you are from around here," Nancy said.

I knocked on Mom's door, and she opened the door, she said, "Russ, you are family. You do not need to knock. Just come in and call out to me." Then she looked past me and saw Nancy. "What's this? You have another young woman on your team? My John is always telling me that he wants to be on your team, as does my boy Russ."

I said, "Nancy will be with us for six months of training, and then she will decide where she wants to work. She is one quarter Texas Indian, but she has lived in the city most of her life. I wanted her to be able to visit you, since she cannot call her parents or friends while she is here. Nancy is a good person, like all the women I know. She will be learning from Jill for a while, and she is my intern in our business of searching for the past.

"By the way, is John Jones home? I will need him to show Nancy the painted rocks and teach her how to be safe in the desert. She also needs to be able to name the wild animals they see and know what plant life will help her survive in the desert. I will talk to John about his desert skills, since he could work to become a team member by teaching us everything he knows about the desert and the sand people. Old and new, and not the cave yet, but maybe a little later."

Turning to Nancy, I said, "Do you understand what you are to start with? First you will work with Jill, whom you will meet when I have everyone come into base camp."

Then I looked at the mountain and said aloud, "Stan and Bob, bring the team into camp."

The master sergeant approached and said, "We have you all hooked up, one tank to the other, and the lieutenant's apartment is ready for her. John Jones watched over your camp while you were in DC. Trucks will be here soon to fill up your water and gas tanks. Look over there toward the mountain—it looks like your call was heard. Here comes Stan, Bob, and Robby."

Nancy asked, "Aren't those two bobcats?"

I said, "Yes, the adult bobcat is Bob, and the smaller cat is Robby, one of her kittens. Stan, the dog, is a good team member, just like Bob and Robby. You will meet Bobby, the other bobcat kitten, when Jill gets here, because he is her bodyguard. Bob is the protector of all life and a punisher of bad people. Stan is a dog of much knowledge who has been in my family an awfully long time."

Stan looked up and asked, "Russ, why do you always describe me as a good dog to everyone you introduce me to?"

Startled, Nancy exclaimed, "Did your dog just talk to you?"

I had to answer "Yes," and Bob and Robby growled softly and said, "You are welcome, Nancy." Then Robby asked, "Can I have her? I will be a good watch cat and bodyguard for her."

"Nancy, you heard Robby," I said. "Will you accept his request?"

Nancy replied, "I have never heard of a cat bodyguard, but let me think about it." Robby walked up to her, bumped her knee, jumped into her lap, and started purring like a cat. "Why is he so friendly?" she asked.

"Because his brother is a bodyguard, and Robby wants to be a better one," I explained. "One day he will be able to read your body language, and you will learn his. If you take him on, he will not leave your side. So, keep an eye on him, learn a little cat language, and grow with the team."

June and Angel came up the trail in the truck. Manuel, arriving on the motorbike, said, "John and Jill should be here in about two hours."

Nancy asked, "Where have they all been, and what were they doing?"

"They were watching the site, as ordered by your boss," I said.

"But how did they know that we had arrived here?" she asked.

I said, "I told them."

Then she asked, "How did you tell them?"

Looking directly in her eyes, said, "You saw me with the flies in DC, didn't you?"

"Yes, but I thought that was a trick," Nancy replied. Then she thought, *oh my, what have I volunteered for?*

June promptly answered aloud, "You've volunteered for the wonders of life on this wonderful world."

Amazed, Nancy turned to June and asked, "How did you do that?"

June answered with thought, *"I am sorry, Nancy. We are not supposed to do what I just did. Please forgive my intrusion into your mind."*

"Will I be able to do that after my internship is complete?" asked Nancy.

"There is a good possibility that you will," said June. "Just pay attention to Russ and Pete."

Meanwhile Pete, John, and Manuel were packing for the trip into the cave. Russ was talking to John Jones about his responsibilities as a team member in case that is what John decided to do with his life.

I told John Jones that his first assignment was to watch the cave opening while we were inside. John would be with me, and Pete and

Manuel would be in the sacred cave studying everything that they could find. So, prepare yourself for your watch," I told John Jones, "and take Bob with you. Stan will be with Angel and June, and Bobby and Robby will be watching over Nancy and Jill."

As we began our day trip into the cave, we left John Jones at the cave entrance with Bob. While John and I went into the cave leading us to the big room of this path into the underworld, Pete and Manuel were in the sacred cave removing the mats of the dead. First, they took samples of the material from which the body covers were made. Then Pete took out his small core drill and started taking core samples of the long bones of the legs, while Manuel worked on sampling the teeth of the dead and looking for DNA. Samples from the body covers, bones, and teeth were placed in sample jars marked by the number in the photo of the bones. Then they covered the remains by the number placed on the dead, packed up what they had brought in, and left the sacred cave to return to the outer world.

Meeting John Jones at the cave opening, Manuel asked, "How long have we been in the cave?"

John Jones answered, "Only three days. Where are Russ and John?"

"They went deeper into the cave," Pete said, "so you and Bob wait here until they come out. By the way, who has been feeding you, Bob or the women at base camp?"

John Jones said, "Both."

Meanwhile John and I had continued our hike into the cave's large room to visit with the chief of the Chichimecs. After our greeting, I said by thought, *"This man is Pete's son John, and he is here in place of his father. From time to time, he and his brother, Manuel, will be coming to visit with you."*

The chief replied in the same manner, *"I have seen into their minds, and they are trustworthy in my mind. But you have other team members whom I have never met, and they may not come here until they agree to accept our rules. They are the ones you call Jill and Nancy and the man John Jones, who is waiting for you at our eastern doorway. Until he accepts the rules, he cannot pass beyond his sacred cave. He has been there many times, but they are not people of the underworld. Where are you going, Russ Philips? Can you tell me? I cannot see that part of your mind."*

"I am continuing my search for the sacred items of the ancient world in

the upperworld," I told the chief in my mind. *"If I return to the underworld, you will be the first to know. I will send the message that you taught me to use, and I thank you for that blessing from your god Zotz, the bat god of caves. Also, I have some new team members to train, while the rest of the team does research on old myths and legends. Then we might have time to introduce you to the complete team, even the cats and dog."*

The chief answered the same way, *"Yes, the dog is smart. I have seen what the cats are capable of from the minds of you and Jill in your camp in the Upper World. We will wait to see your friends and the new ones. I know that you are looking for the Aztec treasure, and that you will help us get payment from the Aztecs for what they did to my people."*

John and I were escorted back to the sacred cave, where we said our goodbyes. Then we continued to the surface, where we were met by June, John Jones, and a well-known air force officer, Captain Lewis.

June said, "The two of you have been in the cave two weeks, Russ. Captain Lewis arrived two days ago with a dispatch for your eyes only."

"It is good to see you upperworld people for a change," I said, "and we were gone for only two days. Hello, Captain Lewis! What brings you to this part of the earth?"

"Well, I have this dispatch for your eyes only," he explained.

I said, "Let us get back to camp, and I will read it with a little food and some water. John and I are hungry."

We loaded the pickup for the ride back. As we pulled into camp, I saw the two airmen who always traveled with the captain sitting at the camp table, which made me think that the dispatch must be important. Taking a cup of water with me, I went into the lab alone to read it. When June brought me a sandwich, I said, "Please call the whole team to camp. I need to talk to everyone about this dispatch, including Captain Lewis and his crew."

The captain stepped into the lab and asked if they could return to Tucson, but I said, "No, your mission is not complete. You and your crew have orders to remain with the team for our next operation. Your next assignment will be in civilian clothing, and you will be required to remain armed. A helicopter will be landing here in a day or two, as I told DC where I would be working and about how long I would be in the cave."

The captain asked, "How did he know when you would be returning to the surface?"

"I told him a long time ago that time passes differently in the cave," I explained. "One day up here is equal to one week down there, so he had a good idea when I would be back on the surface."

As the team began to arrive at camp, Captain Lewis asked, "How did you call them back to your base camp?"

"That is one thing that you will learn today," I answered. Looking north, I saw a dusty road, which told me that the FBI part of the team was almost there. Agent Davis and his partner, Agent Samson, arrived dressed for fieldwork and fully briefed on why they were there. We did not have room for everyone in our lab and meeting tent, so we gathered around the camp tables. I brought out the bottle and glass and set them on the table. Looking around, I noticed that one man was missing.

Pete asked, "Russ, can we get this meeting started?"

"Not yet, Pete," I replied. "We are still one person short."

Then we heard the siren as he sped down the road, and soon the tribal police officer walked into camp. Pointing to his collar and the new silver bars there, he saluted and said, "Lieutenant Juan Wipismal [hummingbird] reporting as ordered, sir."

"I see the tribal council has done the right thing for you and your family," I said. "Okay, everyone, let us get down to the business of this meeting. Why are the air force, the FBI, the tribal police officer representing the tribal council, and our new interns meeting with our team? Mike Garcia is being trained at the university, so he is exempt from all knowledge of this next project. Nancy, you have been extended and will become a full team member today. I have new orders from your commander, and I hope you will decide to stay. Captain Lewis, you and your two airmen know your orders, and I feel confident that you three will stay. I have not forgotten you, Agents Davis, and Samson, who have your orders and came dressed for the job. John Jones, you also will become a team member today if you agree to do so. Now all of you that I have called out will come over to me and I will prepare your minds and bodies for the task ahead."

Agent Davis said, "I now understand what you meant by 'Be careful what you wish for.' Now that we are here, Agent Samson and I are ready to follow your orders."

Nancy said, "I too will follow orders."

I said, "Here on this table, I have the bottle and glass. One by one, each of you will step up here and I will pour you a glass to drink. This bottle and glass will help you quickly learn what you will need to know, including the method by which we communicate with each other. You will learn how to talk to wildlife, including plants, and transfer thought to others. So, step up and drink what the bottle gives to the glass for you."

When Captain Lewis took the glass, it said, "Drink," and he did. "That tastes like water," he commented.

Next came the two airmen, Juan, Nancy, John Jones, Agent Davis, Agent Samson, and all the new members. And finally, June, Pete, Angel, John Garcia, Manuel Garcia, the three bobcats, Jill, Stan, and me. We now had a team of twenty-one members.

Juan asked, "How did you get twenty-one ounces from that half pint?"

"Look at the bottle," I replied. "How did it get full? Now, if anyone has questions, you will have answers within the next twenty-four hours."

"When can we eat?" someone asked.

John Jones spoke up and said, "Mom and the village are cooking us a meal for tonight."

"Are you sure?" I asked. "How do you know, since you have not left this meeting?"

John Jones said, "It just came to me. There will also be fresh meat for the cats and dog."

"Until supper, we will talk about what we are going to do now that we have grown in size," I said to everyone using my thoughts.

The new team member reacted to hearing my thoughts and thought *"Wow!"*

I said, *"You must remember not to explore our minds when we are sleeping, unless you have permission to do so. You will soon learn the difference between personal thoughts and emergency calls for help, as well as what each of us is working on. We will have another meeting in the morning, after a good supper and a good night's sleep."*

Nancy asked, "What is that coming up the road?"

"I hope it is the sleeping quarters for the new team members," I said. "It sounds like the master sergeant's truck with a load. John Jones, would you please tell Mom that we are going to have more visitors today?"

John Jones asked if we could call him JJ, and I said, "Okay, you are now JJ." Then he asked why he could not get Mom's attention using just his thoughts. "Mom is not able to read your thoughts at this distance," I explained, "and she is not connected to your mind now. I am not sure that she will ever be, but when her children were growing up, she could read their thoughts. Do you remember that? For now, you will need to go to her and tell her that more people are coming."

Just then, the words *"Russ, she already knows"* came into my mind.

I said to the group, "Start asking questions in your minds, so that you will start getting answers tomorrow." Then the master sergeant and his crew arrived and started assembling sleeping quarters for the new team members and a larger tent for a conference room with tables and chairs.

The next day we received another dispatch, this time from the general with the flies around his head. I said, "I guess he is pissed at me for making him look like the fool that he is in that meeting in Washington with all those self-centered types who think they know what is best for them."

His name was Major General David J. Johnson, and he and his people would be arriving at Tucson Air Force Base. I was to have Captain Lewis meet them there and bring them to our work site. The bad part was that my team was being replaced by Johnson's military and scientific team. Eighteen members of my team were to be fired, though I was to remain on the site to take Johnson and his scientists into the cave.

So, I called another meeting of my team and told them about the second dispatch—that the government had fired all eighteen team members, as well as all the insects and other critters that had been helping us do our job. "Pack up everything that is yours, but none of the project files on site," I said.

My friend the tribal police officer said, "The tribal council is not going to like this. I am on my way to talk with them now."

I went outside to tell Captain Lewis that Major General David J. Johnson was taking over the site and that he had ordered the captain and Lieutenant Nancy Green to meet him at the air base in Tucson. "My team is packing up to move back to our homes," I told him. "I will be remaining to pass on command to the general. Remember, your abilities are limited to a noticeably short length of time. Your capacity will return to normal first, followed by Lieutenant Green's. You should both be careful with your knowledge and how you use what you know. My advice is to tell the general that you just started this job and know nothing, so that he will not expect any miracles from the two of you. Captain Lewis, you and the lieutenant should become part of the military for the meet in Tucson. The general did not send me his time of arrival, so have a safe trip in your vehicle if you have one. June and I will be moving our stuff back home to Ajo, and then I will be back for the changeover."

Captain Lewis and Lieutenant Green did not make it to Tucson, as his transportation departed after he was dropped off at camp. I was following a big blue bus as I returned to turn the site over to the army. The general was yelling about the captain and lieutenant not meeting him at the air force base and about me not being in camp waiting for him.

As I walked toward him, I said, "I am here now. Why are you yelling at these service personnel? You did not specify an arrival time, so I disbanded my team to leave room for yours. All records are in the lab. If you are ready, I will take you on a tour of the area and down into the cave, but you must remember that it is a sacred cave and has been disturbed too much already. Then we will go down into the largest room that I have been in on this project. The cave is narrow, and it is somewhat difficult to walk in some areas. I will show you the paintings on the walls, and I am sure you have the scientist to read them. I think the three of us would be sufficient for this trip."

The general said, "Okay, but understand this. I need to be back in Washington, DC, in three days."

"Three days will be time enough for this trip into the underworld," I said. "I have my rations in my bag and my headgear, lights, and mask. Your equipment is in the lab tent, and the gas masks for your team are also in the lab."

The general barked out some orders about enough equipment, rations, and water for two days. Then he said to me, "Let's get this cave walk done now."

I said, "Your truck and two men—or Captain Lewis and Lieutenant Green—should wait at the entrance for our return to the surface. They know not to go past the sacred cave. We do not want to upset the tribal council with any more disturbance to that first room. They will keep the entrance safe from intruders or members of your team going where they should not be."

We arrived at the entrance and started our trip down into the cave. When we entered the room known to the natives of those tribal lands as a sacred cave, the scientist photographed everything in the room. Then we continued into the cave, walking for a day, and then resting for a while since the general was not in good military shape.

The scientist wanted to stay in the sacred cave for more study, so I told him that DNA specimens were in the lab at base camp, identified by numerical photo markings in the files. "You don't need to work that room again," I advised him. "If you do, you will pay for your actions by the mountain and what is around this place."

The general said, "No more of your hogwash for the ears of me and my team."

"Don't forget about the eyes," I replied.

As we continued into the cave, the general remarked that he noted points of direction on the cave walls. He asked if the way in the way was also out, and said, "That is a nice thing that you did for the team."

I said to the scientist, "Look at the marks and tell me how long ago these paint marks were placed on this cave wall."

As he inspected the paint, taking a chip and putting it in a sample envelope, he said, "This is just an estimate, but I'd say they're at least fifteen hundred years old."

And we continued, I noted that neither man drank much water or ate anything, just like Pete and I had done every time we returned to the surface.

When we came to the first set of wall paintings, the professor went crazy with his camera. I said, "All of these walls are represented in the project files at base camp."

As we continued, I felt the presence of the little people, so I knew that we were not alone as they awaited our arrival in the large room. I said to the general, "Don't do anything that would upset the people waiting in the next room of the cave."

He asked, "What is going on here, Mr. Philips?"

"What you are about to see is top secret," I replied.

As the three of us walked into the great room of the Chichimecs, the chief was sitting on his throne. The general and his man were trapped in the hell of their minds, unable to move or do anything.

I sent my thoughts to the chief. "*These two men and many others have ordered me to bring them into your underworld so that they can take over your underworld. You have fixed their minds so that they can do nothing. I am sorry that I have broken your rules. These men are killers, like the Aztec were in the beginning, but I do not believe that they would eat you. They are looking for weapons from the past to use in the upperworld. I ask you, chief, and you, god Zotz, the bat god of caves, to make their minds unable to remember anything of this cave. Leave them only the knowledge of their youth. You decide what and where you stop this thing from their minds. Let them remain the same until I get them to the surface, but then make it happen to them. I am your friend, and I will never break your rules again. I will take them back to their world without the chance of war with the upperworld.*"

As I guided the two disabled men back down the cave pathway to the surface, I said to the professor, "Look, more wall paintings!"

He replied simply, "I have what I need."

It took us another day of climbing to reach the surface. Just before we emerged, the general said, "Mr. Philips, what has happened to me, and how long were we in this cave?"

I answered, "Just under three days. Here is the sacred cave, so we are just minutes from the desert outside."

When we walked out into the sunlight, my two cave searchers became twenty years old in their minds.

Captain Lewis said, "You were down there for two and a half weeks, and the general is in big trouble over this takeover."

"I don't think so," I said. "Watch them. They are not in their right minds. I will be on my way home now, back to my wife and pets. Jill has Bobby, and Robby is with Bob at home in my backyard, as free as can be. Stan is playing with all the cats, and Jill has moved into our spare room. Captain Lewis, you are in charge here until you are relieved. If I am ever needed, you know where to find me—somewhere near my home. I will be standing by."

About the Author

This author has traveled the world working at sea and ashore in the navy. He is well versed in the works and has performed from nuclear bombs, ship engineering, to hospitals, and combat sickbays. He also worked in the oil fields of Gulf of Mexico and the offshore oil rigs off the coast of New England. He was consulted by several nuclear power companies, fossil power in project management, construction, and outage management. He had taught in middle schools and had trained offshore employees in performing their duties—correctly and safely. He also helped in designing construction roadways, lite rails, bridges and city parks.

Printed in the United States
by Baker & Taylor Publisher Services